A sp...
alpha ...

Hell Squad: Theron

For a special
#1 Hacketteer,
Amy.

Anna Hackett

Anna Hackett

CW01336053

Theron

Published by Anna Hackett
Copyright 2017 by Anna Hackett
Cover by Melody Simmons of eBookindiecovers
Edits by Tanya Saari

ISBN (eBook): 978-1-925539-20-2
ISBN (paperback): 978-1-925539-23-3

This book is a work of fiction. All names, characters, places and incidents are either the product of the author's imagination or are used fictitiously. Any resemblance to actual persons, events or places is coincidental. No part of this book may be reproduced, scanned, or distributed in any printed or electronic form.

What readers are saying about Anna's Science Fiction Romance

At Star's End – One of Library Journal's Best E-Original Romances for 2014

Return to Dark Earth – One of Library Journal's Best E-Original Books for 2015 and two-time SFR Galaxy Awards winner

The Phoenix Adventures – SFR Galaxy Award Winner for Most Fun New Series and "Why Isn't This a Movie?" Series

Beneath a Trojan Moon – SFR Galaxy Award Winner and RWAus Ella Award Winner

Hell Squad – Amazon Bestselling Science Fiction Romance Series and SFR Galaxy Award for best Post-Apocalypse for Readers who don't like Post-Apocalypse

The Anomaly Series – #1 Amazon Action Adventure Romance Bestseller

"Like Indiana Jones meets Star Wars. A treasure hunt with a steamy romance." – SFF Dragon, review of *Among Galactic Ruins*

"Strap in, enjoy the heat of romance and the daring of this group of space travellers!" – Di, Top 500 Amazon Reviewer, review of *At Star's End*

"High action and adventure surrounding an impossible treasure hunt kept me reading until late in the night." – Jen, That's What I'm Talking About, review of *Beyond Galaxy's Edge*

"Action, danger, aliens, romance – yup, it's another great book from Anna Hackett!" – Book Gannet Reviews, review of *Hell Squad: Marcus*

Don't miss out! For updates about new releases, action romance info, free books, and other fun stuff, sign up for my VIP mailing list and get your *free box set* containing three action-packed romances.

Visit here to get started:
www.annahackettbooks.com

Chapter One

"Race you to the top."

Theron Wade watched his squad mate and best friend, Sienna Rossi, clap her chalky hands together, sending up a cloud of white dust. They were in the Enclave gym, standing in front of a large climbing wall.

Usually, they'd be out fighting the aliens who'd invaded the Earth a year and a half before. But while their squad was on standby, there'd been no mission that morning, and Sienna had challenged him to some climbing.

She smiled at him. That was Sienna. Always happy and sunny. Even after the invasion and all the destruction and fighting, she was like a ray of sunshine. He still remembered the first day he'd seen her among the panicked and shell-shocked survivors milling around at Blue Mountain Base. She'd been calming crying kids and touching people's shoulders.

Today, she had her curly, dark hair clasped at the back of her neck, and her curvy little body covered in black leggings and a purple tank top.

Theron grunted, slapping some chalk on his own

hands. He wasn't supposed to be concerned with what she was wearing, or what was beneath her clothes.

Sienna faced the climbing wall, crouching a little and stretching her neck from side to side. "Loser owes the winner ice cream." Her nose wrinkled. "I know you'll want chocolate ice cream with nothing on it, but when I win, Big T, you'll owe me an ice-cream sundae. With the works. Whipped cream, chocolate syrup, and sprinkles."

Sienna and her damn sprinkles. She was addicted to them. He was listening to her words, but his gaze was drawn to her body again. Her tight workout gear highlighted her curves, and when she bent over to stretch, he had a perfect view of her ass.

He jerked his gaze away. "How do you stay in shape when you're always eating chocolate and ice cream?"

She wiggled her curvy butt and grinned at him, clipping the safety line on the wall onto her belt. "I've got a good metabolism, and I train hard." She reached over and clipped his line on. "Ready?"

He nodded, but before he focused, she shot away, climbing up the wall like a spider.

Theron cursed and followed her. She was the best climber on their squad. Fast, nimble, and fearless.

"La miglior difesa è l'attacco," she called back.

He loved it when she spoke Italian with that lyrical accent. She spouted enough of her mother's and grandmother's sayings that he'd started to pick up a little of the language. "The best defense is a good attack?"

"*Sì*!"

She was well ahead of him as he scaled the wall. She moved steadily, finding each hold and pulling herself upward.

"You'll have to move faster than that!" She laughed down at him.

The sound speared into him. He glanced up, and again his gaze went straight to the perfect curve of her ass. He imagined peeling that stretchy fabric off her, uncovering smooth, bronze skin. He imagined his big hands palming those curves.

Theron's foot slipped. He muttered a curse and regained his footing. He heard her laugh once more. He continued moving upward, but ahead of him, Sienna crowed with glee as she reached the top.

"I win!" She grinned down at him, her face flushed. Just how she looked in his nighttime fantasies when he'd finished fucking her.

Blowing out a harsh breath, Theron paused beside her.

He didn't remember when he'd started wanting her. Most days it felt like forever.

"Now, I'm going to test out these little babies." She pulled out a pair of black gloves. He saw the palms of them were shiny as she pulled them on.

"What are they?" he asked.

"Experimental climbing gloves. Noah Kim and his team made them for me." She lifted her gloved hands and wiggled her fingers. "I've nicknamed them gecko gloves. They have synthetic adhesion, that mimics how a gecko sticks to a wall." She reached down and unclipped her safety line.

Theron's heart kicked his ribs. "Sienna." Noah and his team of genius geeks were good, but it was still a long fall.

"It's fine." She pressed her palms to the smooth wall between handholds...and stuck there like a gecko. She flashed him another smile and started climbing down.

Yeah, he wanted Sienna. But he couldn't touch her.

There were so many reasons why. She was his squad mate, his best friend, and on top of all that, she was sweet and kind and light, and he...wasn't.

Theron knew himself pretty well. He wasn't a talkative, easygoing man, and he had...darker tastes. Tastes that would leave sweet Sienna horrified. No, he wouldn't be good for her. She needed a nice, regular guy who'd do everything she wanted and make her smile.

"Theron?"

He looked down and realized she'd reached the bottom. She was watching him, her brown eyes narrowed.

He grunted, reached for his belt, and let out his safety line. He zipped down to the ground.

"Are you okay?" She pressed a hand to his arm. "You've been edgy lately."

"It's been quiet." He shrugged a shoulder. "Aliens are laying low since the last confrontation, and it's been too long since I had a good fight."

She nodded, but didn't look convinced. She walked over to their things, stripped off her gloves, grabbed a towel, and mopped her face. "We need to find a way to stop this *oura* device."

He grabbed his own towel, and blotted the perspiration away. She wasn't wrong. The *oura* was an alien globe the Gizzida had developed that could control human minds. They'd both seen it used on their friends during the last alien attack. The squads had managed to bring one of the functioning gold globes in, and he knew the geeks in the tech squad were doing their best to figure out how it worked, and find a way to nullify the globe's effects.

"What we need is to find this secret weapon of theirs," he countered.

The *oura* was a problem, but they had an even bigger one. The squads had very vague intel that the aliens had invented some sort of secret weapon. A weapon capable of wiping out the last surviving pockets of humanity.

There weren't that many humans left. Survivors had huddled together in places like the Enclave, and other military bases around the world. They were fighting to survive, and they were fighting back. Theron had dedicated himself completely to his squad, and to fighting the Gizzida.

His way of making up for fucking up. His muscles locked, darkness rising in his chest. For not saving his family, or his fellow Army Rangers.

"God, I wish we knew what it was," she said.

Her voice snapped him out of his black thoughts.

He moved over to a small fridge by the wall and grabbed a couple of bottles of water. He tossed her one.

He needed to focus on his job, but first, he needed to blow off some steam. He decided he'd head back to his quarters and pound his punching bag for an hour or five. Then he'd shower and jerk off. He'd imagine his hand sinking into Sienna's curls and holding her still as he fucked her mouth.

Shit. He wasn't touching Sienna. There was no way he was going to ruin their friendship, or their working relationship.

She was too important to him.

***

Sienna slung her towel around her neck and watched Theron.

Her squad mate was huge, over six-and-a-half feet tall, with broad shoulders and muscular arms. He could bench press her. She knew because they'd tried it once, in front of the rest of their squad, laughing with them.

Theron didn't say a lot and tended to stay in the background. But once you got a good look at his rugged face and steady hazel eyes, he caught your attention. He had this way of looking at you like he was cataloguing everything about you—inside and out. She watched him rub the towel over brown hair that was neither long nor short.

She could imagine him as a big, quiet teen, running herd on his foster brothers and sisters.

He'd told her bits and pieces about being adopted at five, and all the other kids his parents had fostered. Sienna knew that steady, solid Theron would have been the perfect protective big brother.

His gaze flicked her way, and she caught a glimpse of the starburst gold in the green before he quickly looked away.

She frowned. Her friend wasn't acting like his usual self. To most people in the Enclave, he probably looked no different than normal. But she sensed a fine tension vibrating in him, the stiff way he held himself. For a big man, Theron was usually pretty graceful.

He tipped his water bottle back and her gaze zoomed in on his throat, watching as the muscles worked. His damp gray T-shirt clung to his perfectly formed muscles.

Sienna felt a curl of heat through her belly. It was official. She was lusting after her best friend.

And she knew he wanted to fuck her brains out.

She let out a shuddering breath and took a cooling sip of her own water. She was still reeling from that revelation. And he didn't know that she knew.

It had happened during the Enclave Christmas party a few days ago. Theron had stormed out of the gathering, and she'd followed his grumpy, antisocial ass back to his quarters, planning to drag him back to the celebration.

Instead, she found herself standing at the door to his room, watching as he pulled a large—a very large and very hard—cock out of his trousers and stroked himself.

She'd been frozen, watching those long pulls, desire flaring in her hard and fast. She'd instantly gone damp between her thighs, and when Theron had come, he'd called out her name.

Sienna blew out a breath. She'd stood there trembling, turned on, and shocked that this was her *friend*. Shocked that she'd wanted to slide to her knees in front of him and take him inside her mouth, and drink every drop of what he had to offer.

"The aliens will attack soon," Theron said, startling her out of her dirty musings, his voice a deep rumble.

She nodded, trying to refocus on their conversation. "General Holmes and Niko have every drone in the air, searching for any sign of the *oura*, or clues about this mysterious weapon." She hoped to hell Theron couldn't tell that her voice was huskier than usual.

He gave a single nod. His face reminded her of granite—tough and unshakable. Looking at him now, she couldn't tell that this was the man who'd called her name as he'd orgasmed.

Maybe the night of the party had been an aberration? He'd never said anything, or gave her any indication he was attracted to her. Sienna was used to guys showing interest.

She sighed and set her water down. Usually nice guys. She was pretty and cute, and she'd never had to work hard to get a boyfriend. But the attraction never lasted. The guys she'd been with, especially since the invasion, couldn't seem to make sense of her. Pretty woman and soldier. They just couldn't accept her as both.

It was the story of her life. So she liked nice things and could also handle a carbine. She liked colored sprinkles on her ice cream, and could also kill a man in about thirty different ways.

She'd confused her family, too. Her big, sprawling Italian family had been all about togetherness, babies, and food. Everyone had known everyone else's business. Her mother had wanted Sienna to take over the family restaurant in Rome. Her older sister had three kids and another on the way, and her younger sister had just gotten engaged, when the aliens had attacked.

Intense sadness hit Sienna like a ballistic round. God, her sweet nieces and nephews. Her family. Rome had been heavily bombarded during the early waves of the invasion. As far as Sienna knew, her entire family had perished.

It had taken her a long time to accept the fact that they were all gone, now. The pain was a hard ball in her chest that never quite went away. But her squad had helped. All the members of Squad Nine had become her family. They'd helped fill the gaping hole inside her.

And that included Theron.

She remembered that day he'd staggered into Blue Mountain Base. He'd fought through several raptor patrols just to make it there. He'd been covered in blood, and he'd looked so alone, so broken. She now knew he'd lost his family that horrible day.

Theron was the first person she could just sit with and either talk and talk, or enjoy companionable silence...and it always felt right.

But as she looked up at him—the man she'd depended on and trusted with her life for the last eighteen months—she realized she needed something more from him.

Except for the two of them, the gym was empty, and Sienna decided it was time for her to finally test the waters. She yanked her tank top over her head.

A sharp hiss of breath. "What are you doing?"

She grabbed a towel, blotting at her chest. "I'm hot and sweaty."

He was staring at her. No, he was staring at the sexy black whisper of lace she wore.

She cocked her hip. "What do you think of the lingerie?"

"Put your top back on."

She pouted at him. "Don't you like it? It was a mysterious gift from a Secret Santa. You should see the panties." Liking the shocked panic on his face, she hooked her thumb in the waistband of her sports leggings.

A big hand clamped on hers. "Sienna." A warning tone.

She looked up and froze. The gold in his hazel eyes had intensified, and his face was taut and strained. A rush of heat flooded her belly.

"Most guys think I'm into pastel lace—pink,

baby-blue, seafoam—but someone thought this suited me better. What do you think?"

He just stared at her.

"Theron?" she murmured.

He inched closer, heat pouring off his big body. She felt the coiled tension in him, like he was about to explode into action. Like he was about to yank her into his chest and finally touch her.

All of a sudden, the gym doors flew open, and Mackenna Carides strode in.

The second-in-command of their squad was even shorter than Sienna, but every inch of her was tightly packed muscle. Mac had no trouble putting any of the male soldiers on their ass during training.

"Roth wants everyone in the squad locker room," Mac said. "Now."

Theron backed away from Sienna. "We have a mission?"

Sienna sighed and grabbed her tank, yanking it back over her head. "Did the drones find something?"

Mac nodded. "Apparently. I don't have all the details yet. Five minutes." The dark-haired woman strode for the door. "I have to drag Cam out of the pool. See you there."

Sienna straightened her tank. Theron had turned away from her, gathering his things, pretending nothing had happened.

She stared at his wide, muscled back. There was something between them, something he was ignoring, and something she couldn't resist.

It was time she decided exactly what she wanted to do about Theron Wade. She just wasn't sure what the hell that was yet.

Chapter Two

They met the rest of the squad in their locker room.

Theron strode to his locker. Their leader, Roth Masters, was already in his armor, checking his carbine. Around him, the women of Squad Nine were readying themselves for their mission. Mac was pulling her armor on, her face set and quiet. Taylor Cates was beside her, smiling to herself as she got dressed. Since the woman had recently shacked up with former spy Devlin Gray, the brunette had been smiling a lot.

"God, I can't wait to get outside. I've been going crazy in here." Camryn McNabb's voice was edged with a tiny hint of a Scottish accent, and her short, dark hair was still damp. The tall, dark-skinned woman wouldn't have looked out of place striding down some catwalk. But as she slammed her armor on, you couldn't miss the fact that she was a soldier to the bone.

Theron fell into his pre-mission routine, pulling out his armor and weapon. With all the chatter, he could almost be back at his childhood home in Sydney's northern suburbs. Surrounded by a gaggle of foster siblings, his mother laughing in the background and his father watching with a smile. Damn, he missed them.

He pulled his upper armor on, and shoved the painful memories aside. He glanced at Sienna and felt that now-familiar spiky knot in his gut. *No, dammit.*

He listened to the women talking around him. Cam making a snarky comment that had the others laughing. He'd never minded being on a squad with mostly women. He'd worked with lots of soldiers in the Coalition Army, and some of the elite with the Rangers, but the ladies of Squad Nine were some of the best he'd ever fought beside.

"Okay, listen up," Roth called out. "We've been tasked with checking on some survivors holed up in a town not far from here. The last drone flyover showed limited movement in their camp."

"How come these people didn't want to live at the Enclave?" Sienna asked.

"They're anti-government," Roth answered. "Most are older folks who didn't want to leave their homes and farms. And they didn't trust our former president."

Theron heard the acid in Roth's tone. Everyone knew the sordid story of President Howell. The leader of the United Coalition of Countries had sold out mankind to the aliens in return for his own private little Enclave, and his own safety. But more than that, he'd sold out Avery Stillman, a former intelligence agent who'd been trying to stop him, and the woman Roth was in love with.

Of course, the Enclave was now under the

leadership of General Adam Holmes and Nikolai Ivanov. Now, it was a sanctuary for any humans who needed it. Howell had met his own grisly end when he'd been snatched by some flying alien bugs.

Couldn't have happened to a nicer guy. Theron's finger caressed his carbine. He fucking hated bullies.

Soon, the squad was following Roth through the corridor leading to the northeast exit.

Sienna was walking ahead of Theron, her curves now hidden under her armor. But that didn't stop Theron's screwed-up mind from wondering whether she was still wearing that sexy, black underwear under the carbon fiber. Underwear he'd given to her.

He'd known she'd look good in it. For all her sweetness, she was also sexy as hell.

Blake, for God's sake, get a grip. She's your friend. He was grateful when he stepped outside, squinting in the sunlight, and he pressed the button to have his retractable combat helmet slide into place. Theron didn't mind living underground, especially with the Enclave's state-of-the-art artificial lighting system and all the other amenities. It was far more luxurious than their old home, Blue Mountain Base. He liked to stay tucked away in his own quarters, reading, or beating the crap out of his punching bag. His father had taught him to box, and it was in his blood. But there was definitely something to be said about having the sun on your face.

"Let's go." Roth gestured. "It won't take us long

to get to the town on foot."

They started jogging through the knee-high grass. All around were gently rolling, green hills, dotted with small stands of trees. This area, south of the former Coalition capital Sydney and inland of Wollongong, had contained a lot of underground coal mines. One had been repurposed in order to build the Enclave. But topside, there had also been a lot of farms.

"There it is," Mac murmured.

Ahead, Theron saw the town. It had been small, and was made up of a group of abandoned houses and a couple of storefronts. What looked like it had once been a church was now a burned-out shell.

They stepped carefully onto the now-cracked road leading into the town. Roth lifted his hand and gave a signal. The squad stopped in place, and listened. The village was as quiet as a graveyard. They all brought their weapons up. Theron looked down the scope of his carbine, and stepped a little closer to Sienna.

With another sharp signal from Roth, Squad Nine crept forward with the practiced synchronicity of a team that knew each other well. On either side, they were flanked by houses with doors gaping open, and smashed windows. The lawns were all overgrown, and fences sagged.

Theron had visited here once before, on patrol. The survivors lived, grouped together, in just a few of the shops and houses in the very center of the town.

As they turned into the main street of the town,

the destruction became even more pronounced.

From somewhere, he heard the subtle hum of a generator, but his attention was focused on the scorch marks on the buildings, and the overturned cars in the middle of the street. His jaw tightened. The burn marks had been caused by raptor poison.

They moved inside the first shop. Its door was hanging off its hinges, and more burn marks covered the walls. Inside, a horrible smell permeated the air, and Theron breathed through his mouth. He knew that smell. For a second, he was back on the day of the invasion, running to his parents' house, praying they'd be alive.

In the middle of the room was a pile of burned bodies.

"Goddammit!" Roth turned and slammed his boot into the wall.

Theron stared, frozen, at the remains of the people who'd fought for nothing more than to survive. They'd ended up just like his family.

"Theron? Hey?"

He blinked and looked down into Sienna's brown eyes.

"You okay?" she murmured, her brow furrowed.

He nodded. No, he wasn't, but he'd do his job.

Roth sucked in a deep breath. "Break into pairs and search the place. Look for survivors."

As always, Theron and Sienna moved off together. He saw her scanning the street, sadness evident in her dark eyes. They moved up to one of the houses, clearing it in a matter of seconds. When they met in the hallway, she looked at him expectantly. He shook his head.

They moved through two more houses, all eerily empty. In the last house, Sienna turned, eyeing the pink curtains still hanging in one of the bedrooms, flapping in the breeze coming through the broken window.

"Everything good always gets destroyed," she said quietly.

"That's not true."

She let out a sigh. "When you see wanton destruction and death like this, day after day, it makes it hard to believe in the good."

"Yeah." He paused. "I told you that I went to my parents' house during the invasion."

She looked at him. "Yes. But you never told me what you found there."

"Pretty much the same thing we found here. The raptors burned the house down. My parents' bodies were in the yard. They'd obviously been trying to save their foster kids. Raptors had burned them all to a crisp." He knew his voice sounded wooden, like a robot mechanically repeating facts.

"Theron." She grabbed his arm. "You should have told me. Talked about it."

"I was too late to save them." He didn't tell her that he'd disobeyed orders to go there, and abandoned his fellow Rangers during the fight. By the time he'd gotten back to the city, his friends, the men and women he'd vowed to fight with, were all dead, too. "I heard rumors about General Holmes setting up Blue Mountain Base, and decided to take a chance. There were so many dead and dying." His voice cracked. "Then I saw you."

Her face softened. "I remember."

He reached out and grabbed her ponytail, giving it a gentle tug. "And I realized that not all of the good things were gone. There's good at the Enclave." There was good in her. "I see it every time I look at you."

She looked up at him, shock on her face. "Theron—"

Dammit. What part of stay away from her didn't he understand? He took a step back.

Suddenly, he saw a shadow move behind her, darting from one room to the next. He lifted his carbine, and jerked his head.

Instantly, she clicked to attention and lifted her own weapon. "What was it?" A quiet murmur.

"Not sure."

He moved down the hall, aware of Sienna one step behind him. He trusted her to have his back. He reached the room where he'd seen the shadow enter. It was the kitchen.

Theron turned slowly, taking in the old cabinets and scarred countertops. The fridge door hung open, jars and containers smashed on the floor, and the wooden dining table drunkenly tilted to one side because of a broken leg. The room appeared empty.

The back door was also ajar.

Sienna pointed and nudged it open. She looked outside and gasped. "What the hell is that?"

He moved up behind her as she stepped outside. Attached to the house was some sort of orange growth. It looked like a cocoon that pulsed with an amber glow, and had organic tendrils spreading out of it, both up onto the roof, and down into the tall grass.

Sienna stood beside it. The pod was about half her size. She looked back at him. "We should—"

A creature burst out of the nearby shadows.

Theron knocked Sienna out of the creature's path. He opened fire, laser hitting the animal.

The small, four-legged creature growled, jaws snapping. It was about the size of a dog, with glowing red eyes that dominated its face. It was covered in a strange mix of fur, and tough, scaled skin.

Theron kept firing, but the small beast kept coming. It leaped and slammed into Theron's chest. He stumbled backward.

"No, you don't." Sienna jammed the butt of her carbine into the animal's back. It fell to the ground, and the two of them opened fire on it.

With a final yowl, the animal died.

Theron stood there, chest heaving, staring at the twisted remains. It wasn't a canid or hellion—the aliens' rabid hunting dogs.

Sienna crouched beside it.

"Careful," he said.

She touched the creature with her gloved hand and her face looked sad again. "Theron, I think it was a dog. A real, regular dog." She looked up. "It somehow got infected with alien DNA, and turned into a hybrid."

Something good touched by something bad.

They'd witnessed the alien-humans the Gizzida created in their labs. The raptors liked shoving captured humans into their so-called genesis tanks, and morphing them into monsters.

But they hadn't seen alien-animal hybrids before. Why waste a genesis tank on a dog?

"Sienna? Theron? You guys okay?" Roth's deep voice in their earpieces.

Theron touched a finger to his ear. "Just had a run-in with some sort of hybrid dog. It's down, but there is also some strange alien pod here."

"We saw one too," Roth answered. "Got some pics to take back for the team to analyze."

"Acknowledged. We're on our way back."

"Any sign of survivors?" Roth asked.

Theron's gaze met Sienna's. "No."

***

Sienna followed her squad as they trudged back through the fields. The mood of the entire group was somber. For a second, she paused, looking out over the hills. The view was beautiful, and that beauty seemed like such a wrong, stark contrast.

What they'd just left behind hurt her heart, and made it damn hard to acknowledge any beauty in the world right now.

Her gaze moved over a rocky hill nearby. There were no trees, but the hill was overgrown with grass, and topped by a small cluster of boulders near the top. She frowned.

"What?" Theron asked from beside her.

Her frown deepened. She could just see something fluttering in the wind. Fabric, maybe? "There's something up there. On top of the rocks."

Roth flanked her on the other side, yanking a pair of binocs off his belt. He lifted them up, turning the tiny dial until he got them in focus. "There is something up there."

Sienna shoved her carbine onto her back. "I'll climb up."

She reached the rocks, smoothing her gloved hands across the stone until she found a handhold. It wasn't very steep, and she started up, easily ascending the slope.

As always, climbing helped clear her head, and pushed back the horror of what they'd seen in the town.

She reached the top and pulled herself over the edge. She looked down and spotted Theron staring up at her, his gaze intense. He was right below her, no doubt ready to catch her if she fell.

Sienna turned and studied the flat ledge. What she saw made her gut cramp.

"You'd better come up and see this," she called down to the others.

A couple of minutes later, Roth and Theron pulled themselves onto the ledge. Their big bodies crowded in close to her. Theron brushed against her arm, and she was very conscious of his big form. It seemed she was always conscious of him lately.

"You made that look easy," Roth said, blowing out a breath.

"She's a damn good climber," Theron added.

She fought back a flush at the compliment. "Thanks. Now, look at this." She pointed.

The men turned, both of them scowling and cursing under their breath.

"A nest?" Theron said.

"A camp." Sienna studied the burnt-out remains of a small fire, a ratty blanket, and a small pile of trash. Then she looked over the field beyond. "If someone hunkered down here, they'd have a perfect view of the Enclave entrances and exits."

Roth cursed. "How the hell did they manage to evade the drones? Mac, I need the camera." The woman appeared a second later. She pulled out a camera and started snapping images of the camp.

Roth pressed a finger to his ear. "Arden? Do you copy?"

Sienna was dimly aware of Roth reporting their find back to their comms officer. Arden was an integral member of their team. But the quiet and capable woman kept herself apart, rarely socializing with them. At first, Sienna thought they were just a bit rough for Arden, but she'd learned that the woman had lost her husband and children in the invasion, and now Sienna believed Arden didn't let anyone close.

Theron crouched down beside the little nest of abandoned goods. "Looks like there was only one person here."

Sienna nodded in agreement. "And look." She kicked a boot through the small, picked-clean skeletons of some tiny animals. "I don't see any vegetable or fruit scraps."

Theron's face hardened. "Raptor."

The invading aliens were all carnivores. "Or some sort of hybrid."

"It looks like whoever was here is gone now," Roth said.

Theron stood. "Or moved to a new location."

Roth paused for a second, head tilted, clearly listening to whatever Arden was telling him. "Okay." Their leader raised his voice so the others below could hear as well. "Holmes wants us to take a look around, and search for any other signs of our *visitor.*"

Sienna climbed back down the rocky slope, and soon the squad fanned out, searching through the long grass and nearby trees. Although she didn't think they'd find any aliens hiding in the trees. For a reason they still hadn't worked out, the aliens hated the trees. They had some sort of allergic reaction to something the trees emitted.

Finally, with a muttered curse, Roth called them back together. "No sign of anything. I'm not sure we're going to be able to do this alone."

What? Sienna glanced at Theron, and he shrugged.

"I called in for some help," Roth continued, his gaze moving over toward the closest entrance back into the Enclave.

Sienna turned to look over her shoulder. She watched a figure step out of a hidden doorway. The woman was wearing simple, dark clothes, but her white hair stood out like starlight, and matched her pale skin. She strode toward them, a large black bird resting on her shoulder.

Chapter Three

At first glance, Theron thought that Selena could pass for human. But up close, you could see her skin and hair were too pale, and her eyes were larger and a bright, non-human green.

Cam pushed forward. "God. He's not a little fluffball anymore, is he?"

Selena smiled, waving a hand at the bird perched on her shoulder. "He's growing fast, and getting bigger every day. Something the Gizzida did to him causes accelerated growth. I still call him Fluffy, though. The name's stuck."

She had a soft, melodious voice, and as she spoke, the bird flapped his wings a little. He'd just been a chick when he'd been rescued, but he'd lost his fluff and now his skin was black and looked like leather.

The alien gyr chick came from Selena's world—a planet who opposed the Gizzida—and they'd both been snatched by the aliens. Fluffy had been subjected to various experiments, and according to Selena no longer resembled the gyr birds from her world. But after Finn, one of their best Hawk pilots, had rescued Fluffy, Selena had taken him in, and now the chick was one happy little guy.

"You think he can track down our spy?" Roth asked.

Selena nodded. "Do you have something from the camp you found?"

Roth handed over a ragged scrap of cloth that had been torn off the blanket. Selena took it, and held the fabric up to Fluffy's face.

Then, she said something in her strange alien language, and the bird took off in a flap of wings.

Theron arched his neck to watch the bird slice through the air, the dark shape circling around the blue sky. Fluffy sure was quick. The creature zoomed downward, and landed at the camp on top of the rocky hill. Then he lifted off again, dipping and flying on the wind.

"He loves flying," Selena said. "He doesn't get out enough." The alien woman closed her eyes, breathing deep like she was absorbing the sunshine and the fresh air.

Theron felt a spurt of anger. Another being abused by the aliens. He'd grown up being bullied for being the adopted kid, and later he'd seen his foster siblings bullied, too. Until he was big enough to stop it. He hated anyone who took advantage of someone weaker than themselves.

They all watched the bird and Theron felt a prickle on the back of his neck. Someone, or something, was out there. "My gut's telling me someone is watching us."

Selena walked forward, heading toward the area underneath where the bird was flying. Squad Nine followed behind her, and that's when Theron noticed something. He nudged Sienna and pointed, and when she saw what he was indicating, her mouth dropped open.

The grass beneath the alien woman's feet was growing—right before their eyes. He knew Selena had some sort of affinity with nature, but as he stared at the grass, rippling and unfurling in front of him, he realized knowing and seeing it were two different things.

The bird circled over their heads.

"He doesn't seem to be finding anything," Sienna said.

"No," Selena agreed.

Theron hoped it stayed that way. Hopefully, their uninvited visitor was gone.

Then Fluffy swooped in and landed back on Selena's shoulder. She pulled something out of her pocket and held it up—some sort of bug—and the gyr quickly snapped it up. Selena murmured something to him, and the bird nuzzled her cheek.

"So, no raptors?" Roth asked.

"Unfortunately, he's detecting a presence, but whoever they are, they are well hidden."

All the soldiers froze. *Damn.* Theron gripped his carbine tighter and looked around. Yeah, he'd known.

Suddenly, his earpiece crackled to life. "Squad Nine." Arden's crisp voice. "Security cameras have picked up a raptor heading for the western Enclave entrance. Squad Nine respond."

Goddammit. Theron swiveled, and felt the others tense around him.

"Cam, get Selena back inside," Roth ordered.

The alien woman shook her head. There was fear in her green eyes, but she lifted her chin. "No, I might be able to help. And I don't want to deprive you of a soldier."

"I don't have time to argue," Roth said. "Stay back, and let us do our job."

Selena nodded. Together, they all ran toward the western entrance, weapons up. They rounded a stand of trees and ahead, Theron saw the tall form of a lone raptor, standing with his back to them.

The squad ran in, circling the tall being. The alien was over six-and-a-half feet, with a humanoid body that was all hard-packed muscle and thick, gray-mottled, scaly skin. Prominent brow ridges and a heavy, elongated jaw with very sharp teeth dominated his frightening face.

Sensing them, he turned and stared at them. His eyes glowed deep red.

"Scans are showing no more raptors in the vicinity," Arden said.

That couldn't be right? Why send in just one alien? Theron scanned their surroundings. This had to be a trap.

Suddenly, another team of Enclave security personnel came out of another entrance, headed by Captain Kate Scott. The woman was head of the security team, and a seasoned soldier.

They all stood there for a long moment, weapons trained on the lone raptor. Around them, the sun shone down, and birds tweeted in a nearby tree.

The raptor didn't move.

One of Captain Scott's security team members held up a small scanner. "No explosives present."

Or at least nothing they could detect. Theron angled his body closer to Sienna.

"On your knees," Roth said.

The alien responded, dropping to his knees and holding his hands up.

"Why are you here?" Roth asked, carbine aimed at the raptor's head.

"To warn you." The alien's English was perfect. "My name is Gaz'da."

Theron frowned. That sounded familiar.

Suddenly, Roth lowered his carbine. "You were in the cells at Blue Mountain Base. With Captain Bladon. You helped us."

The raptor nodded. "And I hope to help you again." His burning red gaze moved over them, touching Theron's for a second. "Before it's too late."

***

Sienna knew that this raptor was an ally, but that didn't stop her from keeping a tight hold on her carbine.

She walked directly behind Gaz'da, as they led him inside and toward the holding cells.

Ahead, a door opened and a tall redhead stepped out into the hall. She was wearing a uniform, her hair pulled back in a braid. When she saw the alien, she gasped and moved forward.

"Gaz'da." She held a hand out.

The alien gently took her hand in his larger, clawed one. "It is a pleasure to see you again, Laura."

Captain Laura Bladon had run the prison cells and interrogation team at Blue Mountain Base before they'd been forced to evacuate it when the aliens had attacked. Now, she did the same at the Enclave. But, as far as Sienna knew, the cells were currently empty.

Laura led the alien inside and over to a table. She waved to one of her team members, and the young man brought the raptor a glass of water.

Sienna and the rest of her squad moved back against the wall, but didn't leave. They all wanted to hear what the alien had to say.

A moment later, a tall, commanding man in uniform entered. General Adam Holmes had an aristocratic face and a touch of gray at his temples. He was a general to the core, and it was thanks to him that any of the Blue Mountain Base survivors were still alive.

A second man came in right behind him. She watched Nikolai Ivanov's gaze swing straight to Mac. Mac shot her lover a tiny smile. Sienna had to admit, she was more than a little envious of her friend. Niko, a former-spy-turned-civilian-leader of the Enclave, was one long, dark, sexy, Russian drink of water. Add in the fact that he was an artist, and Mac often had streaks of paint in interesting places on her body, and it was enough to make Sienna sigh in envy. Her gaze slid to Theron and lingered.

Not now. She forced her gaze back to the alien.

"You've been watching us," Laura said.

Gaz'da nodded. "I saw the attack here, and my brethren's device. After their defeat, I followed them to gain more information."

"You went back to them?" Laura asked quietly. "I told you to get away."

Sienna swallowed. She'd assumed Gaz'da had escaped during the Blue Mountain Base attack. It appeared he'd had a little help. She knew he'd been like them once—an enemy of the Gizzida. He'd been captured by them, and forcibly turned into a raptor.

Gaz'da's face contorted. "I couldn't run. Besides, I have nowhere to go." A bleak look crossed through his red eyes. "At least if I help you, I feel I am fighting back in some way." The muscles in his face rippled. "They ruined my life, as well."

With a shock, Sienna felt a prick of tears in her eyes. It was so horrible. This being was alone, with no way to get back to the homeworld he barely remembered. That any species thought they had the right to overtake another planet and forcibly change people into something else made her feel sick.

Whatever happened in their fight against the aliens, Sienna vowed she would die fighting. She would not be changed. She glanced at Theron beside her. And whatever happened, she was damn well going to grab life by the horns and experience everything she could.

"Do you know what this secret weapon is?" Holmes asked.

"No." Gaz'da sipped his water, the glass looking like a toy in his huge claws. "But I know that the Gizzida are working on one. And they are doing something in one of the tall towers in your city. They are building a large *oura* there, to lure people out. One large enough to cover the entire city."

Curses erupted around the room.

"What about glowing orange pods?" Roth asked. "We saw some in the town near here."

Gaz'da shook his head. "I do not know."

Holmes stepped forward. "Laura, can you put a call through to Noah? Tell him to get down here. I need an update on the *oura* work."

The woman nodded and moved to a nearby comp. Sienna saw Noah's hawkish face flash up on the screen. He shot Laura a wide grin. "Hello, my dragon. Miss me already? I hated leaving you all warm and naked in our bed this morning."

Laura rolled her eyes. "Room full of people, Kim. Including the general and Niko."

Noah looked unrepentant. "Pretty sure they know we're banging each other's brains out."

"Stop it." Laura's cheeks were pink, but she looked like she was fighting a smile. "The general needs you down here for an update on the *oura*."

Mention of the *oura* wiped the smile off Noah's face. "On my way."

Moments later, the head of the tech team strode into the cells. One look at him was enough to know why Laura was happy to share the man's bed.

Noah was tall, and walked like a man used to getting his way. His black hair brushed his shoulders, and framed a face that showed his South Korean heritage. Because of him and his team, they had lights, hot water, and functioning weapons.

There was a woman Sienna didn't know standing beside him. She was small, with messy blonde curls that looked like she'd cut them herself. She had a pretty face, but her baggy clothes hid her body.

Noah saw Gaz'da and stopped. "Gaz'da."

The alien inclined his head.

"Noah," Holmes said from the table. "Gaz'da returned with intel for us. How close are you to nullifying the effects of the *oura*?"

Noah shook his head. "Not there yet. Damn thing isn't like anything I've seen before. Marin, here, has been helping me."

"We aren't getting very far." The woman had a surprisingly deep, whiskey-toned voice. "I have created a set of goggles, but it only stops the effects of the *oura* light for a couple of minutes, at best." Her nose wrinkled. "The rest of the tech team are sick of being used as guinea pigs."

"A few minutes are better than nothing," Roth said.

Marin nodded, her curls bobbing. "I'll get some sets of them issued to you." She glanced at Gaz'da. "Any additional information we could get would help."

"I will tell you everything I know," Gaz'da said. "But it isn't much."

"He has told us that there is something going on in a tower in the city," Niko added, his gaze meeting the general's. "I suggest we divert all available drones into the city. Find whatever tower they're working in."

"Then we can plan a mission to go in," Roth said. "Destroy their *oura*, and gather more intel on this secret weapon."

Holmes nodded. "Agreed." He looked at the alien. "Thank you, Gaz'da." Then he looked at Roth and the squad. "Squad Nine, I need you on standby for this mission. As soon as we know what tower the aliens are in, and what the hell they are doing, I want you to go in."

Sienna felt a surge of energy. *Good.* A plan of action. They could get in there and destroy this globe, and maybe finally find out what this weapon was, and how to stop it.

Chapter Four

Sienna was vaguely aware of Roth and Mac talking as the squad left the cells. They were already prepping so they'd be ready when the mission got a green light.

The group headed back to the upper levels of the Enclave, and the usual itchy feeling spread through Sienna. She wanted to be out there *now*. Waiting sucked.

They turned into another corridor, and the sound of hammers banging and some sort of saw buzzing caught her attention. She glanced over into a side tunnel and saw construction work going on.

Since they'd taken in more human survivors in the last week, accommodation in the Enclave was getting a bit tight. Niko had a team in charge of creating and outfitting more quarters.

One of the contractors looked up. He had shaggy blond hair, worn jeans that hugged a fine body, and a toolbelt around his waist. Yes, Mike screamed "hot builder", and he and Sienna had indulged in some flirting here and there. He'd asked her out a few times, but just lately, she hadn't really been interested.

She now knew that the reason that Mr. Hot

Builder wasn't doing it for her was because of the big man right behind her. That wasn't Mike's fault, though. She lifted a hand and waved at the man as they passed.

Out of the corner of her eye, she saw Theron scowl. Sienna blew out a breath. How come she was attracted to Mr. Scowly, instead? But she knew for all his tough exterior, Theron had a good, protective heart inside him. So, how the hell did she get Mr. Scowly to touch her?

They reached the locker room, and as everyone got changed, Roth turned to face them, his hands on his hips. "Be ready. As soon as we have the intel we need, we'll go in."

"Darkswifts?" Mac asked.

Roth nodded.

Sienna set the last of her armor back in her locker and tugged her T-shirt back in place.

"You dating that guy?"

Sienna turned to see Theron glaring at her. She shrugged. "He's asked me out."

"What happened to the schoolteacher?"

She closed her locker door. "It didn't work out. Like so many of the guys I've dated before, all he wanted to do was wrap me up in cotton wool." The moron had suggested she quit her squad. *Idiot.* "They don't seem to understand me." Hell, maybe she didn't understand herself. The common denominator to all her failed relationships was her.

"They want to change you," Theron grumbled. "Make you match the pretty picture of you that they have in their heads."

"Yes." Damn, he'd hit the nail on the head.

"Saw a version of it growing up. Couples would be interested in adopting some of my foster siblings. But they wanted the cute kids, not too big or too small, or too noisy or too quiet. Everyone had this perfect image of the kid they wanted."

Her throat tightened. Poor Theron, seeing what had happened to his family. No wonder he spent so much time in his quarters, or the gym, pounding on a punching bag.

"No one seems to realize that I can be a woman and a soldier at the same time. I like to cook, and gorge on ice cream, and I also like bringing an enemy alien down." She took a step closer until they were only an inch apart. "And I can be a sexy woman who likes it hot and sweaty in bed."

She saw Theron's nostrils flare.

Bait thrown, Big T. She patted his shoulder and walked out of the locker room, grinning. Her mood much improved, she headed down the corridor with a bounce in her step and naughty thoughts in her head.

So, she wasn't expecting it when someone reached out and grabbed her arm from behind, tugging her into a side tunnel. Hands spun her, and she came face-to-face with Mr. Hot Builder.

Annoyance spiked. "Mike."

"I've been waiting for you." Mike reached up and ran a finger down her arm. "We've been dancing around each other for days. I'm tired of it, doll."

Doll? Sienna gave an inner sigh. She pushed his hand away, and tried to think through how she could get out of this without causing a scene. The Enclave was a small place.

"Look, I'm sorry, Mike. I wanted to be sure that I wanted to date you, and, honestly, I just don't think we'd fit."

Instead of backing away, Mike clamped his hand around her wrist. "I think we'd fit just fine."

Sienna gritted her teeth. If he didn't back off, she was going to break his damn wrist. She yanked on her arm. "Let me go," she said calmly.

"Come on, Sienna. A pretty thing like you needs a man." He backed her up against the wall. "Someone to spoil you and keep you warm at night."

Yeah, she wanted a man, but not an asshole. She opened her mouth to blast him—

A big form appeared beside them, and suddenly Mike was dragged away from her. He gave a sharp cry.

"What the fu—?"

When Theron spun the man around, Mike's words cut off. Sienna looked at Theron's face. His barely-leashed rage was evident in the granite-hard line of his jaw.

He slammed Mike into the opposite wall.

"You don't touch her." Theron's voice was a deep growl. "If she says to let her go, you let her go."

His dark tone made Sienna shiver. Theron didn't lose it often, but when he did... She hurried forward. Time to defuse this situation.

"Hey?" She grabbed Theron's muscled arm. "Let him go, Big T. He's not worth it."

Theron didn't budge.

She sighed. "Please." Under her fingers, his muscles tensed, but then he released the man.

Mike stumbled back. "Bitch. You could've just said no. You didn't need to sic your guard dog on me."

Sienna's own anger spiked. She grabbed his wrist and twisted his arm. He went down to his knees with a yelp. "Pretty sure I said no quite a few times, asshole." So much for not making a scene. She rounded on her friend. "Theron, what the hell was that?"

He scowled. "That asshole grabbed you—"

Mike made a pained sound. "Hey—"

She bent his arm more, ignoring his choking noise. "And you didn't think I could handle it?"

Theron's scowl deepened. "He—"

"I'm not delicate." She cut him off. "I'm not some damsel for you to rescue, or kid for you to protect."

"I know that."

"I don't think you do." She poked him in the chest. "I'm not sure you really see me at all." As she said the words, a sharp stab of disappointment filled her.

Something flared in Theron's hazel eyes. "Don't turn this around. He's bigger than you. Stronger."

"And I'm a trained soldier."

"With no armor on. It's different."

She felt anger ignite. "You think the only reason I'm good at my job is because of my armor?"

"Will...you let me go?" Mike choked out.

Sienna blinked. She'd forgotten about the jerk.

She released him and he shot to his feet. Rubbing his wrist, he shot them both a dark look and scurried off.

She looked back at Theron. "You didn't think I could handle that?"

All of a sudden, Theron moved—fast. She knew he could do that when he wanted to. He grabbed her and yanked her hard against him. Her breasts were pressed against his rock-hard chest, and all the air raced out of her lungs.

"I know you, Sienna. You wouldn't have wanted to hurt him or cause a scene."

She pushed against Theron, but he didn't budge.

He leaned down, his breath warm on her cheek. "You think that once he smelled you, he'd stop? Once he felt how you'd fit against him, with that sweet little body, that he'd let you go?"

Desire flowed into her, need making her belly tight. His voice was a sexy rasp, his body so hard against hers. "Theron."

"Stop me," he growled.

She lifted her head, their gazes locking. Something dark and edgy ignited in his eyes, something that was a twin to what was inside her.

She shoved against him, and he shoved back. He was physically much stronger, but Sienna knew she was much sneakier when she needed to be.

"What if I don't want to stop you?" she said breathlessly.

He made a growling sound. "I'm not right for you."

"I think we're very right." She sucked in a

breath. God, he smelled so good. "I think we should sleep together."

He jerked against her. "Dammit, Sienna." Then his mouth slammed down on hers.

Ohhh. Oh, wow. She melted into him, pushing up on her toes to get closer. His tongue pushed into her mouth, and she met it with her own, drawing in the raw, male taste of him.

He made a guttural sound, and his arm wrapped around her. She leaped up, wrapping her legs around his waist. He turned, pushing her against the wall. He grabbed her wrists with his free hand and shoved them above her head.

So much passion. As his tongue pushed deeper into her mouth, like he was trying to claim her, need exploded in Sienna. She needed more. She needed closer.

He ground his hips against her, and she felt the hard bulge of his erection. He was feasting on her and shocked pleasure coursed through her. She cried out his name.

And it was like she'd tossed a bucket of icy water over him.

Suddenly, Theron backed off, unwrapping her legs from his waist and stepping away.

Sienna blinked in confusion, glad that the wall was holding her upright.

"I'm sorry," Theron said stiffly.

The wonderful, hot need inside her went cold. "Sorry?"

"I lost my temper."

She stayed against the wall, hurt coursing

through her. "You were mad? That's all this was?"

"Yes. I could've hurt you—"

Sienna cut a hand through the air. "Don't. You wouldn't have hurt me."

"I...have big hands."

"Dammit, Theron. I like my sex hot, sweaty, and hard. Or, at least, I think I do. Everyone's always treating me like a fucking fairy princess." She stomped her foot. "I am *not* a princess."

Theron took a step forward, then stopped. "I care about you. You're one of my closest friends and I only want what's best for you."

"*I* know what's best for me." She *thought* she did, at any rate. She knew that the world wasn't the place it had been before the invasion. She knew that every moment was precious, especially for those of them on the squads. Any day could be their last.

She wanted to try everything, discover what felt good and made her happy. And she wanted to know what being held by Theron felt like. She wanted to kiss him, feel the passion that flared between them, brighter than anything she'd felt before.

Theron shook his head. "I'm just as bad as that asshole who touched you."

"I didn't want him to touch me."

Theron just stared at her and said nothing.

"I know you want me," she said baldly.

Now, he shook his head.

"I deserve some honesty," she said. "You're my friend. I *saw* you."

He went still. "Saw me?"

"During the Christmas party. In your room—" her breath hitched at the memory "—stroking yourself."

He went rigid, his face turning to stone. But he remained silent.

Sienna swallowed. "Theron, say something."

More stubborn silence.

Theron was nothing, if not stubborn. She'd always joked and called him as hard and unyielding as a rock. He could outwait anybody and if he'd decided he wasn't going to discuss this, he wouldn't.

"I want you, Theron."

More silence.

Pain sliced through her. Suddenly, Sienna was exhausted. If he really wanted her, if he really cared, he'd do or say something.

His silence was answer enough. "We're meeting the others for a late lunch in the dining room shortly. I'll see you there."

He gave her a stiff nod, spun on his heel, and walked away.

Sienna sagged against the wall. She felt wrung out.

She stared down the corridor after Theron, then lifted a hand and rubbed her aching chest.

But she wasn't giving up. Stubborn Theron hadn't seen anything yet.

***

Theron sat beside Roth at their usual table in the

dining room. A general hubbub of conversation filled the air, punctuated by the tinkle of knives and forks hitting plates. Food at the Enclave was pretty darn good, and President Howell had made sure the place was outfitted with the best. Theron glanced at the fancy plates. Meals here were sure a lot prettier than at Blue Mountain Base.

And yet, even knowing that, he couldn't do much more than stare at the food on his plate without a hell of a lot of interest.

Exhaling softly, he admitted the truth to himself. He was waiting for Sienna to arrive.

I think we should sleep together.

He knew he was in a grumpy mood. It was partly because that builder asshole had put his hands on her. But it was the rest of the conversation, as well.

Knowing that Sienna had watched him jerk off while he fantasized about her... Shit. He'd promised himself he'd protect her, and never go there with her...and now it was all he could think about.

He heard a familiar laugh, and his head snapped up. Sienna entered the room, with Taylor and Cam. The three women—each deadly and gorgeous in their own way—made quite a sight. He saw plenty of guys in the dining room look up and watch them.

When they reached the table, he expected Sienna to sit beside him like she always did. But when she ignored him and sat on the other side of the table beside Mac, he felt the stab of hurt. He guessed he deserved it.

Theron had learned pretty quickly in life to be honest with himself. He'd had a rough start, but then he'd gotten lucky when his parents had adopted him. They'd given him a warm, steady home, and a place where he could be himself. Where he could learn about himself. Theron knew what lived in his blood, and he never planned to get married or have kids. He also knew what he liked in bed, although he hadn't had sex since the invasion. He'd known that fast, hurried tumbles with scared and lonely women wouldn't even start to scratch his itch, and finding someone who shared his tastes wasn't easy.

Oh, but he'd fantasized. The problem was, his hand was a poor substitute for what he really wanted.

And he knew what he wanted wasn't what Sienna would want. He refused to jeopardize their friendship in any way.

"What's got you looking so down?" Roth asked.

"Nothing." Theron picked up his homebrewed beer and sipped it. Since they were on standby, he could only have one beer, and not the whiskey that he'd prefer.

Roth lifted a brow. "Woman trouble, huh?"

Theron hunched his shoulders. The last thing he wanted to do was tell his leader that he was lusting after one of their squad members. "I'm steering clear of her."

Now his friend smiled. "I tried that. Want some advice?"

Theron turned his head. If Roth knew Theron was lusting after Sienna, the man would have a fit. Sure, the rules had all been thrown out the window after the invasion. He knew there were couples on other squads, like Shaw and Claudia on Hell Squad.

But Theron wasn't the long-term-relationship kind. If he touched Sienna...no, it would ruin everything.

"Not sure I want your advice," Theron said. "I seem to recall you screwing up pretty badly with Avery for a really long time."

"Because I was an idiot. I should have listened to her more, and not been so pigheaded."

Across the table, Sienna laughed at something Cam said. He stared at her expressive face and watched as she dumped colored sprinkles on top of her ice cream. She loved the damn things, and her stash jar looked like it was almost empty. She always gave him a hard time about liking his ice cream plain.

He tried to imagine telling her what he wanted. That he liked rough sex. That he got turned on when a woman pretended to struggle and when she let him tie her up and talk dirty.

Yeah, right. She might like to say she liked it hot and sweaty, but there was something so fresh and innocent about Sienna Rossi.

"Ladies." The deep, rough voice made Theron glance over. Tane and Hemi Rahia were standing by their table.

The two men were from Squad Three, known to

everyone as the berserkers. Made up of bikers and former mercenaries, the berserkers were rough, wild, and deadly on the battlefield. Theron had never seen anyone go into battle laughing, the way these guys did.

Tane was the leader, and his brother Hemi, his second in command. The taller, leaner Tane had an unsmiling face and long dreadlocked hair. Hemi was built like a tank and covered in tattoos.

"We're on our way to the games room," Hemi said. "Thought I'd challenge Squad Nine to some epic battles of pool." He waggled his eyebrows.

Cam snorted. "We whipped your ass last time, Rahia."

Hemi's gaze hit the other woman, and it instantly turned hot. Theron had been watching Hemi circling Cam, and Cam doing her best to shut him down, even though anyone with half a brain could tell the two of them were on fire for each other. Cam had issues she didn't freely share with anyone else. Theron hoped Hemi could find a way through the woman's tough shell.

"Maybe," Hemi conceded. "But since I enjoyed it, it doesn't count."

Cam snorted again and grabbed her drink. She stood. "All right, then. But we're betting this time. Clothing credits. I have my eye on a new bikini."

As Hemi's gaze clouded over, Theron suppressed the need to shake his head. Cam knew just how to play the man.

"Did someone say pool?"

Theron felt someone lean into him and looked

up. Michelle was a survivor from Blue Mountain Base. The woman was a little older than Theron, liked lifting weights, worked on the maintenance staff...and made him some tempting offers a time or two.

He felt someone looking at him and glanced across the table. Sienna was watching him with a steady gaze and a blank face.

Decision made, he stood. "Sure thing. Grab a drink, and let's go have some fun."

Michelle grinned and linked her arm through his. "I like fun."

Chapter Five

Sienna sat at the small bar in the games room. There was no bartender at work here, you just helped yourself to something from the cooler, and cleaned up your own mess. Since they were on standby she was having a soda, but she really wanted something alcoholic. Something to dull the pain.

She looked over toward the pool tables. Cam and Hemi were locked in an epic battle, and trading insults. Tane and Roth were having a civilized game at the next pool table. And Michelle was flirting with Theron at the third table. She was leaning into him with her big, strong body, laughing her loud, full-throated laugh. He wasn't really flirting, and his face was its usual granite mask, but he didn't seem to mind her standing so close.

Theron was a real gentleman when it came to sex. If he'd been with anyone, he'd never mentioned it. She watched Michelle smile at him and he leaned in to take a shot.

He was thinking of sleeping with her. Sienna was sure of it. She ran a finger down her glass. She was getting his message loud and clear.

"You look like someone stole your favorite sprinkles." Mac slid onto the chair beside her.

"It's nothing. Over and done with now."

"Man trouble."

Sienna lifted her glass. "Isn't it always? You snagged a good one. Handsome and sexy as hell, who liked you from the start and wasn't afraid to show it."

Mac poured herself her own soda. "It wasn't exactly smooth sailing, Sienna. Relationships take work, effort, compromise. Especially when that person is a friend, and someone you work with every day."

Sienna realized she'd been staring at Theron, and jerked her gaze back. "It's nothing."

Mac rattled the ice in her drink. "It doesn't look like nothing. And the way he watches you when you aren't looking isn't nothing."

He watched her? Sienna's chest hitched, and then she stomped down on the reaction. "He thinks I'm not right for him."

"Most people think Theron is the strong, silent type," Mac said. "And he is, but he's also pretty in touch with himself and what he likes. I've always liked that about him."

Sienna nodded. "He had a good family and was tight with his mom and dad. And they had a big foster family...sounds like a pretty good place to learn what you like." Pain rose in her throat. "Apparently, that's not me."

Mac watched her for a long moment. "You sure you want him? Or is he just forbidden fruit?"

An old saying of her nonna's drifted through Sienna's head. *I frutti proibiti sono i più dolci.* Forbidden fruit is the sweetest.

Mac tilted her head, her gaze direct. "A man like Theron takes what's his. Once he's claimed it, he'll never let it go. Doing so would shatter something inside him."

Sienna knew that. It was part of what she liked most about him, his unshakeable values and sense of right and wrong. It was why she knew he felt so guilty about the death of his Ranger team. "I want him, Mac. I can feel the pull between us and I think it's something special."

Her friend nodded. "So, what are you going to do about it?"

"Nothing, if the bonehead sleeps with that woman," Sienna growled. Michelle was leaning over to take a shot, wiggling her ass at Theron. "He's put me in some neatly labelled little box. Sweet friend and squad mate Sienna. He won't let himself want me."

"Okay. So how are you going to convince him that you won't accept that label?"

"I...don't know." Michelle's booming laugh rang across the room. "I could be more obvious? Dress in something to make him see me? Flirt?"

Mac shook her head. "That's not you. You need to be *you*, your charming, sweet self. Talk to him and show him a little more, the stuff you keep hidden."

"I'm not even sure what I'm hiding." Sienna's fingers tightened on her glass.

"What do you want, above all else?" Mac asked. "And I don't mean the Gizzida gone for good. We all want that. What do you want for *you*?"

"I want someone to love me. All of me. Every corner of my soul."

"Then you need to let him see all those corners, and you need to love every corner of his."

Suddenly, the games room door slammed open, and Arden hurried in. Squad Nine's comms officer was a slim brunette, with pale-brown hair, flawless, creamy skin, and a calm, soothing manner. Sienna always envied Arden's air of elegance, but the woman also carried a deep well of sorrow that was reflected in blue eyes that almost looked violet. Sienna and the others were always trying to get her to join them and have fun, but she always politely turned them down.

Today, she looked a little frazzled.

"Roth," Arden said. "The drone team has picked up something. A sighting of a large *oura* globe."

Sienna slid off her stool. *Finally*.

"In the city?" Roth set his pool cue down. "Have they identified the tower?"

"No." Arden shook her head. "It's in the Blue Mountains."

***

Theron leaped out of the hovering Hawk. As his boots hit the ground, he swung his carbine off his shoulder, and scanned the trees ahead.

He'd missed the scent of the mountains—green

trees and dampness in the air—since they'd left it. Ahead, old, rusted rail lines ran up over the hill, trees crowding in on either side. The sun was setting, washing everything in shades of orange and gold. That also meant night would be on them soon.

As his squad pulled in tight, the Hawk quadcopter rose silently on its thermonuclear engine, its gray metallic body disappearing as its illusion system clicked on.

"Okay, listen up," Roth murmured. "The *oura* was spotted in a large railway salvage yard ahead. We go in, see what the fuck the aliens are up to, and we destroy the *oura*."

They set off, following the tracks. Sienna was moving beside him, her hands steady on her carbine. She was her usual focused self. For a second, he pictured her face as she'd watched him with Michelle back at the Enclave.

He'd hurt her. He watched her try to hide it, but he knew her too well. He'd purposely led Michelle on, and he'd hurt Sienna. *Fuck.* Theron dragged in a deep breath. It was for the best.

"There." Roth murmured through their earpieces.

They'd rounded a curve, the tracks hugging the hillside, and ahead lay a large, dilapidated warehouse, surrounded by scrap. It looked like some sort of train graveyard.

Old, rusted train engines and carriages lay around, a few whole, but most with pieces broken off of them. There were also piles of scavenged metal and wood. Ahead, he saw the workshop was little more than sheets of metal for walls, and a roof with large roller doors that could be opened and closed at one end. There were a few grimy windows dotting the walls.

Roth took the lead, raising his hand to give them signals. They moved in tight formation toward the workshop.

As they skirted around some piles of scrap, Theron saw a flash of yellow through the dirty windows. Roth gave another hand signal, and they all reached for the special goggles that were dangling around their necks.

Theron fitted the goggles over his eyes. Noah and Marin had worked overtime to get the goggles ready and issued to the squads. They limited his visibility a bit, but he'd take that over having his mind under the control of the raptors any day.

Another hand signal. Roth wanted them to split into two groups to circle around the workshop. Theron went left with Sienna and Taylor. Roth took the right with Cam and Mac.

Theron carefully picked his way through the scrap, stepping over the rusted tracks and piles of old parts. They crossed some open ground and he ran fast, reaching the workshop and pressing his back against the sheet-metal wall. Sienna and Taylor were right behind him.

They crept along the building. There was a grimy window ahead, with cracks all through the glass. He caught the faint golden glow and made for the opening, wanting to get a better look at just what the hell they were dealing with.

But as he reached the window, carbine fire and raptor fire broke out inside.

There was the sound of breaking glass, and guttural raptor shouts.

Fuck. Roth had engaged.

Beside him, Sienna and Taylor dropped the stealth. The three of them faced the large window.

He pointed, then backed up a few steps. He started running, and then lifted an arm to shield his face. He jumped through the window, glass shattering around him.

Inside, he landed with a roll and came up firing. He was aware of Sienna and Taylor leaping through the window behind him, and he gave them cover fire.

Across the workshop, he saw Roth, Cam, and Mac taking cover behind some workbenches. They were shooting at a group of raptor soldiers.

Theron kept firing, and then spotted a large shadow coming at them out of the corner of his eye. He spun. A giant raptor was charging at him from behind a piece of equipment. The fucker was close, too close. Theron fired until the last second, and as the alien leaped at him, he dropped his carbine.

As they went down, Theron was ready. Hand-to-hand was his favorite form of fighting. Borne of one-too-many schoolyard scuffles, and his boxing training.

The weight of the raptor drove the breath out of Theron. The bastards were big and goddamn heavy. But Theron jammed his hands up. He had the advantage of the exoskeleton built into his combat armor, which gave him added strength.

They rolled across the dirty floor, bumping into something. Theron finally got on top of the beast, and reached down and yanked his gladius combat knife from its sheath. Several short, powerful stabs, and the raptor fell back beneath him, blood gushing.

Theron leaped back to his feet. As he turned, Sienna was there, handing his carbine back to him. He grabbed it and started to nod his thanks, but she was already spinning away. She went down on one knee and kept firing at the last of the raptors.

Seconds later, all the laser fire stopped.

Every raptor was down. Roth moved through the downed bodies, checking they were all dead.

Then their leader's gaze landed on the large, flat railway wagon ahead. It was loaded with a large object, the size of a car, that was covered in a rough, canvas sheet. Dim, golden light spilled from beneath it.

Squad Nine surrounded the car.

"Keep your goggles on, and try not to look directly at the light for too long," Roth said.

"I am not fucking being caught by that alien mind control shit again," Cam snapped.

Theron knew none of his squad had enjoyed having their brains blanked by the *oura*. Luckily, he and Sienna, along with Tane, Hemi, Devlin, and Taylor, had freed them.

Roth grabbed the end of the sheet and pulled.

Theron hissed out a breath. Beneath the sheet

were three sets of outdoor lights—heavy-duty sets used for night-shift work on construction sites. They'd been colored yellow and plugged into an alien power cube.

He blinked. It wasn't an *oura*. "It's a damn decoy."

"Fuck." Roth shoved his goggles up on top of his combat helmet. "It's just a bunch of yellow lights."

"This was just to get us off the real trail," Sienna said.

Mac stalked forward, grabbed the pulsing raptor cable linking the lights to the power cube and yanked it out. The lights died, leaving the workshop in shadow. Night was falling.

"All right, I'll call in a Hawk," Roth said, his voice tight. "Let's get the hell out of here."

"And find out where the hell they've really got the *oura*," Mac muttered.

Suddenly, there was the sound of something metal falling and hitting the concrete. They all spun and lifted their carbines.

"There!" Sienna shouted.

Theron saw a raptor dart out from behind some equipment and sprint out of a side door.

"Dammit, stop him! Theron and Sienna, go!" Roth ordered.

Theron broke into a run, Sienna right beside him. They charged out the door. Ahead, he could just make out the raptor running down the train tracks and into the darkening night.

They gave chase. Sienna lifted her weapon, firing on the run, but most of the shots went wide.

The raptor jerked once, but didn't slow down.

Theron pulled in air and pushed for more speed. A second later, the raptor took a sharp turn to the left and darted into the trees.

Dammit.

"Follow him," Sienna yelled.

They crashed into the trees, dodging tree trunks. A flicker of satisfaction ran through Theron. The trees would affect the alien and might slow him down.

But, he thought with a frown, if the bastard got away, he could call for reinforcements. They had to wait for the Hawk, and couldn't risk being surrounded.

"I think he went this way." Sienna turned right.

Theron spun to follow her, and tripped over something. He couldn't tell what in the shadows. Cursing, he caught his balance and kept running. But in those brief seconds, he'd lost sight of Sienna.

"Sienna!"

Where the hell was she? He strained to hear anything.

Then carbine fire shattered the twilight.

The blood in his veins turned to ice. He dodged around a tree, and ran as fast as he could.

Theron broke out of the trees and then skidded to a stop. Ahead, lay a large ravine. They were all standing at the top of a steep slope covered in rocks that was a few degrees away from being a cliff.

The raptor was standing at the very edge, teetering, arms windmilling.

Sienna was just a meter away from him, carbine

aimed at the alien's chest. She fired again, and the raptor started to fall backward.

Theron released a breath. *Good riddance.*

But at the last second, the raptor lunged out with a clawed hand. He grabbed the end of Sienna's carbine.

She cursed and was jerked forward. The raptor held on and yanked her over the edge.

"No!" Theron raced forward.

In the growing darkness, he saw the dim shapes of both the raptor and Sienna, tumbling down the steep slope.

Without thinking, Theron jumped over the edge, and started skidding down after her.

Chapter Six

Over and over, the world whirling, Sienna fell down the slope, rocks and sticks jabbing into her.

She felt something catch on the fastening of the armor panel covering her side and then the carbon fiber was ripped away. *Dammit*. She rolled again and landed on something hard, a sharp pain piercing her unprotected side. But she kept rolling and the fall felt like it went on forever.

Then she came to a jarring stop.

With a grunt, she landed hard on her back. She stayed there, stunned and dazed, trying to pull air into her winded lungs. God, she hurt. Despite her armor taking the brunt of the fall, her body was an explosion of aches and pains.

Sienna took stock, moving her arms and legs. It hurt, but nothing was broken…she hoped.

She heard a crashing noise, and her pulse leaped. Damn, she'd forgotten about the raptor. She scrambled around, looking for her carbine, but didn't see it anywhere.

Suddenly, a big body landed beside her. She spun, lifting her fists.

Theron knelt near her. His face was scratched and bleeding.

"Theron."

He crawled over to her. "Sienna. Are you okay?" He gripped her shoulders, powerful hands curling around her.

"A little battered, but I'm fine. Have you seen the raptor?"

Theron looked behind her. "I don't think he'll be a problem."

She turned her head, feeling a sharp pain slice her neck as she did. Her gaze settled on the motionless raptor lying a few meters away. His body was bent at an unnatural angle, his back broken.

She looked back at Theron and groaned. "God, I hurt."

His hands ran down her sides. "Anything broken?"

"I don't think so." She reached down and touched the burning pain on her side. She grimaced and pulled her hand away. "I think I'm bleeding somewhere."

"You lost a piece of your armor."

"Yes." Then her gaze moved to Theron's chest and she gasped. "Theron!"

He glanced down at the sharp stick that was poking right through a joint in his armor and into his chest.

"It's not deep." He grabbed the stick, and yanked it out with one pull.

She gasped. "You shouldn't have done that." She

pressed a hand over the hole, felt the stickiness of blood.

"It's fine. Priority is getting out of here." He pressed a finger to his ear. "Roth? Arden? Do you copy?"

In her own earpiece, Sienna didn't hear anything. She looked back up the slope of the ravine. To the east, she could see stars appearing in the night sky. To the west, the last of the daylight was slowly dying away.

"The ravine's blocking our comms," Theron said, his tone frustrated.

"They'll find us." Roth Masters and Squad Nine never left anyone behind.

Theron helped her to her feet. "We need to move away from here, in case any raptor scum come searching for their friend."

"Any sign of my carbine?" she asked.

They took a few moments to scour the area, but her weapon was gone. Sienna squelched a flash of disappointment. She was used to the weapon, had broken it in, and it had saved her life too many times to count.

Together, she and Theron moved away from the raptor body. Every step was agony for Sienna, but she sucked back the complaints.

"Maybe we'll find somewhere where we can climb up," Theron said.

Sienna eyed the slope. She loved climbing, but the thought of it right now made every part of her ache and throb. "It's too dark. It's far too risky to climb that when we can't see."

Theron nodded. "Come on. Let's keep moving."

The shadows turned to dense darkness at the bottom of the ravine. She wanted to turn on her flashlight, but knew they couldn't risk it. Soon her hip and leg started to protest. She limped, biting back the pain.

A strong arm wrapped around her, taking a lot of her weight. Whatever did or didn't happen between her and Theron, she knew she trusted him with her life.

Their earpieces crackled to life.

"Theron? Sienna?" Roth's deep voice, distorted by static.

"We're here," Theron answered.

Through the comm line, Sienna heard Roth's heavy breathing and the sound of carbine fire. "We're under attack. Raptor reinforcements arrived."

Dammit. Sienna's hands curled into fists. Her friends were fighting, and she and Theron weren't there to help.

"We are in a ravine west of the scrapyard," Theron said. "We can't climb back up. We'll need an evac."

"Acknowledged." A tense silence followed, and Sienna pictured their leader, and the rest of their squad, fighting. "Shit. Another raptor patrol just turned up. The Hawk is inbound. You guys sit tight."

Sienna stared up at the stars. "I hope they're okay."

"They'll be kicking raptor ass," Theron said darkly.

But she heard the same worry in his voice. He wanted to be up there taking down raptors. "How did you end up falling down the slope, too?"

His hazel eyes were shadowed. "I didn't fall."

She sucked in a breath and bit her lip. *He'd come after her.* "You shouldn't have done that." Pride tilted her chin up. "You'll be late back to Michelle now."

His brow creased. "Michelle?"

They stared at each other, tension filling the air between them.

"Theron? Sienna?" Roth was back. "We can't make it down to you guys in the dark. Hole up, and take shelter. Arden says there are no signs of any raptors in the ravine. We'll be back in the morning."

Sienna blew out a breath. She'd suspected as much. The important thing was that their friends were safe and headed home.

"Roger that," Theron said. "See you tomorrow." He looked down at Sienna, and gave her a grim nod. "We're on our own. Let's find some shelter."

With an arm around each other, they limped through the trees. With each step, Sienna felt the flex of his muscles around her torso. But for once, she was too tired and sore to picture what those muscles would look like without his clothes on.

Soon, a familiar sound caught her ear, and she lifted her head. Running water? They came out of the trees, and ahead, Sienna saw a long, narrow waterfall tumbling from above, down into a small pool.

"There's an overhang over there." Theron pointed just adjacent to the spray. "And I think we can risk a flashlight for a bit."

They moved toward the water, and Theron set Sienna down on a rock. With her gaze level with his chest, she could see his wound was still bleeding.

"We need to take a look at your injury." She pulled out the field first aid kit on her belt.

"And I want to check your side. You're favoring it." He flicked on his flashlight, orienting it toward the overhang. "Then we'll eat and get some rest."

She wrinkled her nose. Food meant the ready-to-eat meals that they all carried in their field emergency kits. "Won't be very tasty."

"No, it won't. But it'll help us get by until they come and get us." He moved to the pool, and she watched as he crouched by the water. He carefully peeled his upper armor off. He was wearing a sweat-soaked black T-shirt underneath, and he gripped the back of it and yanked it over his head. Even in the dim light, she had a perfect view of his bare chest.

Every inch of him was muscled. She knew he worked out a lot, and had his beloved punching bag and some weights in his room. Before the invasion, he'd been on the Army boxing team. Not her idea of recreation, but she couldn't argue that she didn't enjoy the results.

As he scooped up some water and splashed it on

his chest, she felt her mouth water. She watched one rivulet run down his pecs, over the ripped ridges of his stomach and into the waistband of the cargo pants he'd been wearing beneath his lower armor.

Dragging in a deep breath, Sienna snatched up her first aid kit and moved over to him. The field kits only had the basics, and she took out some antiseptic wipes and knelt down beside him.

"Let's see that injury, Big T."

He stayed still as she dabbed at the puncture wound on the top right of his chest.

"That must hurt." She tried to focus on the blood and ragged injury, not his sleek skin.

He grunted. "I'll survive."

Sienna cleaned the wound and probed it a little. He didn't make a sound. "Thank God. It isn't too deep."

"Told you."

"Yeah, well, you aren't always right, and I know how stubborn you are." Their gazes clashed for a humming moment, before she looked back at his chest. She pulled out a sealer bandage that would adhere to his skin, and pressed it over the wound. "There you go."

"Now you," he said.

She stood and, with practiced moves, took her upper armor off, stacking it by her feet. She lifted the hem of her beige tank up. Well, it had been beige once. The lower half was now soaked with blood. She winced at the sting. "I think I grazed my hip during the fall."

"It was a hell of a fall." Theron bent down, his face close to her bare belly. She looked up, staring at the dark trees.

"Scrape goes lower. You'll have to take off your trousers."

Great. With methodical movements, she took her lower armor off, and then flicked open her cargo trousers. Theron had bandaged her wounds plenty of times before. This was no different.

Matter-of-factly, she shoved her trousers off, leaving herself standing there in her tank and panties. He seemed frozen for a second, before he gestured to a nearby rock. She sat down, and when Theron moved between her legs, she tried to control the vicious surge of desire that rocketed through her.

He started dabbing at the graze with antiseptic wipes. It stung, and she hissed out a breath. With long, gentle swipes, he followed the graze from her hip down to her left thigh. His touch was gentle. She'd noticed that about Theron. He had big, strong hands, and could be rough and strong when needed, and at other times, so gentle.

He dabbed some more. "Open your legs. This scratch goes down your inner thigh." His voice was thick and raspy.

She closed her eyes and trembled. She couldn't believe she was so turned on by him tending her injury. It was wrong.

She let her legs fall apart.

She sensed him go still. She opened her eyes, looking down at his dark head. He was staring at her black panties.

The breath rushed out of her. "Theron."

***

They were simple black cotton panties. They weren't sexy or provocative, and yet Theron had never seen anything so tempting in his life.

His hand curled around her thigh, and he was careful not to touch the nasty graze that marred her skin.

He lifted his head and big brown eyes looked back at him. In that second, he knew he'd give her anything.

"Sienna—"

"I'm burning up," she murmured.

He saw the flush on her face in the low light. It would be so easy to touch her. To take care of her, to pleasure her, to ease her ache.

His fingers dug into her skin. It would be so easy to take her. And then what? Where would that leave them?

Jesus, she was hurt, and they were stuck here, just the two of them. He shouldn't be thinking of getting Sienna Rossi naked and sliding his hard cock inside her.

He *wasn't* going to touch her.

She bit her lip, her shoulders slumping. "I can see the 'no' in your face."

"Sienna—"

She shook her head, some curls escaping from her ponytail to frame her face. "Forget it, Theron. I think I'd just like to suffer in silence."

Dammit. When she tried to move away from him, he gripped her thigh and held her in place. "We don't fit."

She tilted her head, studying him. "I disagree."

"I'm not the right kind of guy for you."

"You don't think I deserve a steady, quiet, grounded guy? Who knows me better than anyone else? Who I care about?"

He blew out a breath. "I told you I was adopted."

She frowned and nodded.

"My birth mother was a prostitute and a drug addict."

Sienna gasped. "That's terrible. I'm glad you ended up with your parents."

"I was with her for five years, Sienna." He looked down at the hand on her thigh. "I have her hands. Big hands. And she had this horrible laugh." He forced his gaze back to hers. "They took me off her when she tried to sell me."

"Sell you?" Horror was all over her pretty features.

Yeah, in Sienna's big Italian family, kids didn't get sold by their mothers.

Now hot color flooded her cheeks. "She tried to get rid of you? To sell her child? That's reprehensible!"

Theron let out a harsh laugh. "She wasn't trying to get rid of me. She was trying to sell me for sex. To men who liked little boys."

Now, Sienna's face went white. Her hand clamped over his. "No."

"Children's Services got me out before anything happened. That's how I ended up with my parents. My real parents."

Sienna released a breath. "That just makes me more proud of the man you've made yourself, Theron. Not less."

Damn. "I have this darkness inside me, Sienna. It's not good or bad, it just is. You have no darkness. You're good and—"

"Sweet. Ugh. I get it." Her fingers dug into his. "I'm not this paragon of light and virtue you've made me into, Theron. You *know* me. I fight, I get covered in blood and gore, and contrary to what you might think, I have sex. I like it."

"I like rough sex, Sienna. That's my preference. That's what turns me on. Regular sex...it's no more exciting to me than jerking off."

She blinked. "Lots of people like rough—"

He shook his head. "I don't mean against the wall or doing it doggy style. I mean places most people don't go. I mean holding a woman down, spanking her ass until it's pink, I mean tying her up."

Her eyes went round. "You're into BDSM."

"No." He cursed. "I couldn't care less about all the rules and complications. I just know I like it rough."

"Why?" she asked quietly. "Why do you like it?"

He shrugged, feeling like he was fucking walking naked through the dining room at the Enclave. "Does there have to be a why? Sure, life started out shaky, but I had a great family, parents loved each other. I just knew pretty early I liked things a little different when I jacked off while imagining tying up my first girlfriend and ordering her to go down on me."

Sienna swallowed. He saw her trying to process everything and he was so damned glad not to see horror and disgust on her face.

"Do you imagine doing that to me?"

He jerked. *Jesus Christ.* "Sienna...it doesn't matter. We aren't going there. You're my friend, one of the closest I've ever had. I won't touch you."

Beneath his hand, her leg tensed. "Maybe I'll like it."

Quiet words that burrowed under his skin and speared into his gut. He wanted. Oh, yeah, he wanted. But he yanked on the leash he'd put on his desire for Sienna. It was fraying, but it held.

"Show me, Theron," she murmured.

And the leash unraveled a little more, holding on by the tiniest thread. No. He wouldn't touch her, but he could still take care of her, give her something, even if he tortured himself in the process. Just this once.

He let his fingers brush a small circle on her thigh. He watched her squirm a little, her breathing increasing.

"Me touching you turns you on?" he asked, his voice barely more than a growl.

"Yes," the answer came out of her in a rush.

He loved that she was so responsive. "Are you wet?"

She licked her lips, her eyes darkening. "Yes."

"Show me."

She hesitated for a second.

"Show me, Sienna." He let the command bleed into his voice.

She let her legs fall open even wider. She stared at him, waiting for his next order.

Fuck, his cock was hard. He stared at the juncture of her thighs, that sweet part of her hidden by that damn scrap of cotton. Ignoring the voice screaming at him to get up and take a dive into the cold water nearby, he stayed right where he was. "Pull your panties aside."

Her breathing was ragged now, and her hand traveled down her taut belly before reaching the black cotton. She pushed it aside and he hungrily looked at her. She was pretty and pink, and wet and glistening. He wished the light was better so he could see more of her.

"So pretty." His cock was as hard as steel and throbbing under his armor. Need pounded through him and he forced himself to focus on her. "Touch yourself."

This time she didn't hesitate. Her finger moved through her folds, sliding up to circle her clit.

"That's it." God, he wished it was his hand on her, his mouth. "You like that I'm watching you, don't you?"

"Yes." Her touch grew bolder and she started rubbing herself vigorously.

He sucked in a breath. "Put a finger inside yourself."

Sienna arched a little, sliding a digit inside her.

Her gasp echoed in Theron's ears. This was Sienna. *His* Sienna. He'd imagined the sound of her gasp and cries so many times. "How's that feel?"

"Full. Good."

He'd fill her more. Stretch her more. He easily imagined the feeling of sliding inside her. "Faster. Rub your clit."

She did as he ordered, her hips moving. "I'm close." Her white teeth bit down on her plump lip.

"Come, Sienna. Come for me."

She bit down harder, moaning. Then her back arched and her body shook as she came.

She was so damn gorgeous. Theron forced himself to stay where he was, letting the aching throb of his cock be his punishment for letting things go this far.

When she finally blinked and looked at him, he saw her gaze was hot and slumberous.

He shot to his feet. If he didn't move, he'd touch her. "I'll go clean up. Then we'll eat."

He headed for the water. He needed to dunk his head. Hell, maybe his entire body.

"That's it?"

Sienna's voice made him pause. *Fuck.* He should never have done this. He didn't look back at her, his hands clenching into fists. "That's all I have to offer you."

"You are *so* damn stubborn, Theron."

He heard her footsteps, and then he felt her push up against his back, her full breasts pressing into him.

"When are you going to stop lying to yourself? You *want* me."

"I care about you. About us and our friendship." He could smell the sweet smell of her. Not quite vanilla, but something else that made him think of baking and delicious things. His control, already stretched thin, wavered.

"We both want to be more than friends, and you know it." Her hands smoothed up his arms. "You enjoyed that little moment we shared. I enjoyed it. I want you to show me more."

Theron spun fast and heard her gasp. He gripped her chin, forcing her gaze up to his. He had to do something to get her to back off. Because it wouldn't take much to drive him over the edge. Then he'd be pushing her down into the dirt and taking her every way he wanted to.

"I might play with good girls, but they don't do it for me."

He felt her stiffen.

"For me, being with a sweet, sexy thing like you is just foreplay. It doesn't hit me, not deep down where it matters."

She flinched and pulled away from him.

As he stared at her face, he knew that once again he'd wounded her. Far worse than the graze on her side.

He turned and stomped down to the water. Crouching down, he splashed the cool liquid onto his face. He wanted to dive in, but he wouldn't risk it. He looked up at the top of the ravine, lost in the darkness above. Who knew where the raptors were? He wouldn't leave Sienna unprotected.

Besides, he couldn't risk being naked around her.

When he headed back to their makeshift camp under the overhang, she was dressed and sitting with her back against the rock, her knees drawn up to her chest. She was munching on the tasteless field rations. Another packet was sitting near his things.

"You rest first," he said. "I'll take first watch."

There were no smiles or teasing remarks. She simply nodded. When she'd finished eating, she found a flat spot on the ground, turned away from him, and faced the rock.

Theron sat nearby and clicked off the flashlight. He stared out into the night. He'd hurt her. The very thing he'd wanted to avoid.

Shit, she messed him up and left him so turned around he didn't know which way he was facing.

The hours ticked by, and the night turned surprisingly cool. It was the middle of summer, and he'd expected it to be warm.

He heard a small noise and looked over to see that Sienna was shivering. He stared upward, telling himself to leave her. Calling himself all kinds of names, he made his way over to her and lay down beside her. He curled his body around her.

"Theron?" Her voice was drenched in sleep.

"Just rest."

She stayed still for a moment, but didn't pull away. Then he heard her breathing even out again.

He tightened his arm on her. She was so small and so tempting and so damn trusting.

Holding her, he stared at the rock wall and fought for the last dregs of his control that were slowly crumbling away to nothing.

Chapter Seven

Sienna watched the sunrise, and scanned the trees, even as her mind remained lost in her thoughts.

Theron had woken her during the night so they could switch shifts. She'd watched as the eastern rim of the ravine had slowly turned a faint pink, then orange, and then finally day had beaten back the night. He was asleep, sitting up and leaning against the rock wall behind her.

Right now, she didn't even want to look at him.

I might play with good girls, but they don't do it for me. His words had been echoing around in her head for hours. She was attracted to him, felt something deeper for him, but most of all, she wanted him to be happy. If she couldn't make him happy...

She sighed. They all deserved to find some bright piece of shiny in this shitty world they had to call home. A part of her prayed that they would find a way to finally drive the Gizzida away, but another part of her knew what their odds were. And that meant they all needed to find some pleasure in the present—to help get them through...and perhaps because that was all the good they were going to get.

Dammit, she was melancholy this morning. It was time she turned her gaze away from Theron and let their relationship settle back into what they'd had.

Something made her glance up into the sky, and she caught a faint glimmer. A Hawk was incoming.

She turned around to wake Theron, and saw that he was already sitting up, eyes open and staring into the sky as well.

"Looks like our ride's here." Sienna stood, gathering their meager gear.

"Sienna—"

The low rumble of his voice scraped painfully over her skin. She shook her head. "No need to say anything, Big T. I heard you." *Loud and clear.*

She strode out from under the overhang. She didn't want to hear any excuses or apologies. She just wanted to get back to the Enclave and have a hot shower.

The Hawk hovered above the trees, and two zip lines dropped down to them. Sienna clipped one of them onto her belt. Moments later, she was zipping up toward the quadcopter, Theron right behind her. They both climbed aboard.

A blond head poked out from the cockpit. "Morning," Finn Erickson said cheerfully. Then he raised a brow, clearly taking in their serious faces. "Rough night?"

"You could say that." Sienna moved to one of the seats in the front row and dropped down, not looking at Theron. "We fought off raptors, fell down a cliff, bled everywhere, and spent the night outside."

Finn winced. "Fair enough. Let's get you home." He ducked back into the cockpit.

She heard Theron settle in behind her, and then the Hawk was lifting up and banking left. She closed her eyes. Theron had drawn blood with his comments, and now she knew how he really felt.

It was a quiet trip back to the Enclave. Sienna managed to doze briefly, and before she knew it, they were lowering straight down through the retractable doors into the Hawk hangar bay.

She didn't wait for Theron. Sienna leaped up and shoved the side door open. She jumped out, to find Roth waiting for them.

"Are you both okay?"

Sienna nodded. "Can't wait for a shower and some decent food."

Roth's shrewd gaze switched from Sienna to Theron, and back again. "You sure?"

Sienna nodded. "Just scrapes. Everyone else is okay? You guys made it back in one piece?"

"Yeah. Still no word on the *oura*, though."

Right at that moment, Sienna was too tired to care. "I'm going to check in with Medical. I'll see you later." She didn't look at Theron as she strode out of the hangar bay.

Moving on autopilot, she stopped at Medical and let one of the nurses check her graze, then she headed back to her quarters.

She loved her room, and had made it as homey as she could. A while ago, she'd found a framed picture of the Rome skyline that she kept on the wall. In fact, there were a number of little knickknacks she'd collected. At first, picking things up while out on a mission had felt wrong. But now, she thought of it as a way to honor those who hadn't made it. She had a cute little plush winged dragon, a beautiful carved statue of a ballerina, a set of candles she loved burning, and an action figure of some futuristic soldier from a game. His armor looked a lot like what the squad soldiers wore, and his tough face had reminded her of Theron.

She turned her attention away from her décor, and headed for her bathroom. She stripped off, and gratefully stepped under the hot water, thankful for the Enclave's plentiful supply. She spent a long time letting the water beat down over her head. It helped her to not think of anything. To not think of the hot look in Theron's eyes as he demanded she touch herself. The way he watched as she'd come...

I might play with good girls, but they don't do it for me.

Ugh. She shut off the water, and toweled herself dry. How the hell was she supposed to grab some sleep now, when she knew she'd just see Theron in her dreams, watching as she touched herself. She'd just wrapped herself in a towel, when she heard the comm unit by her bed chime.

She hurried out and pressed a button. "Hello?"

"Heard you did some camping."

The deep rumble with a touch of New Zealand in it made her smile. "Hi, Hemi. The camping was not by choice."

"Can't say I like the hard ground or field rations much, myself. Hey, you were down for teaching some of the teens climbing with me today. I'll understand if you're not up for it—"

It was just the distraction she needed. "No problem. Let me get dressed, and I'll meet you in the gym."

"You are a trooper, sweet thing. See you there."

When Sienna strode into the gym, a group of teenagers were huddled by the climbing wall. Hemi was there, and should have looked menacing and intimidating, with his massive muscles and numerous tattoos. But the big guy was grinning, and some of the teens were joking with him. A couple of the girls were even eyeing his ass and giggling.

"Hi, Sienna."

She stopped to smile at the young girl. Clare was a sixteen-year-old that Hell Squad had rescued from some underground train tunnels in the city. Sienna remembered that the girl had been painfully thin, and so timid when she'd arrived at Blue Mountain Base. But she'd started coming out of her shell since they'd arrived at the Enclave.

A boy of about the same age stepped up beside them. Leo was Clare's best friend. They'd survived the tunnels together, and went everywhere together ever since. Leo had started to fill out, hinting at the man he was growing into.

"Hi, Clare. Hi, Leo."

"You've been out on a mission?" Leo asked.

She nodded. "Yep. Theron and I had a small issue chasing down a raptor, and had to spend the night in the mountains."

Clare smiled shyly. "I miss the mountains sometimes."

"I know how you feel, Clare." Sienna moved over to the climbing chalk and coated her hands. "Ready to do some climbing?"

Leo nodded. "Yes. I want to improve my skills. Hemi's brother is giving me carbine lessons down at the firing range after this."

"Tane?"

Leo shook his head. "Ah...no, he scares me a little. Manu."

Sienna smiled. "Manu doesn't scare you? He's even bigger than Tane and Hemi." And ran the firing range with an iron fist. He'd been a berserker, but had been injured on a mission and lost his leg. It had put him off the squad, but it didn't keep the man down.

"Hemi and Manu are...less intense," Leo finished. "And Theron's been giving me boxing lessons. He's a tough teacher."

"He's given me a few lessons, too," Clare said. "He works with a few of the kids."

That was Theron, spending time with these kids who'd lost everyone. "What's with all the lessons?" Sienna asked.

Clare wrinkled her nose. "Leo wants to join the squads."

Leo lifted his chin. "I know I'm not old enough, or had enough training. But one day. I want to help and I want to fight."

Sienna squeezed the boy's arm. "That's honorable, Leo." God, she sure as hell hoped they'd beat the Gizzida long before Leo was old enough to join a squad. She turned to face the group. "Okay, everyone. Time to warm up and get climbing. Let's start with five laps around the gym."

The room echoed with moans and groans, but the teens started jogging around the gym's perimeter. It wasn't long before she and Hemi had them all hooked up and climbing. She couldn't believe that most of the teens were still pretty happy, full of smiles and jokes. Despite most of them having lost their families, despite everything they'd been through, they found some joy. Life still went on.

They were the perfect antidote to her bad mood. She corrected Clare's form, helped another young boy, and called out some tips for those at the top of the wall.

When they all came back down to the bottom, she sent them back up again.

Sienna stood beside Hemi, eyeing his bearded face. No one would call him handsome, but the man exuded sex appeal in spades. He had his big, tattoo-covered arms crossed over his broad chest which was stretching his black T-shirt to the limit.

"Would you sleep with me?" she asked.

He made a choking noise and turned to look at her, his eyes bugging out. "What?"

"It's a hypothetical question. I need a man's opinion."

He recovered his stride. "You sure it's just hypothetical?" He waggled his eyebrows.

She arched one brow. "I know who you really want, Hemi, and it's not me, but if you were unattached—"

"I am unattached."

She snorted. "Okay, if you weren't panting after a certain squad mate of mine."

Hemi gave a single shake of his head. "Sweet thing, you're a gorgeous, sexy woman. Whoever he is, he's an idiot."

She wrapped her arms around her middle. "We can agree on that. On one hand, he thinks he's protecting me and knows what's best for me." That just made her mad. "On the other...I know he wants me...but I don't think he wants me enough."

"Then he's a huge idiot. You want me to beat him up?"

She smiled at Hemi, even though she felt sad. "He said I'm a good girl and wouldn't...be enough for him."

Hemi's face hardened. "Okay, now I really am going to beat him up."

She blew out a gusty sigh. "I guess it's time to give up."

She felt Hemi's gaze on her. "If you want my advice, sounds like it's time to play dirty."

Sienna turned to face him. "Mac said I should be myself."

Hemi snorted. "Bet Mac suggested you 'talk' and 'communicate'."

"Yes. That's what adults generally do."

Hemi snorted again. "It's not what guys do. Guys can turn into idiots, especially when they think they're doing the right thing. Talking and being fair don't get you anywhere."

Sienna turned it over in her head. "You sound awfully wise for a big, wild berserker."

He smiled, that slash of white teeth turning his rugged face somewhere close to attractive. "I can be wild and rough. But I know what I want, and I'm not one to beat around the bush about it." His grin morphed into a scowl. "Even when the woman I want keeps running scared in the opposite direction."

Sienna turned back, keeping an eye on the kids. Cam wasn't a coward, but she was running from Hemi. Something told Sienna that she should put her money on the determined berserker.

"You sure this guy is worth it?" Hemi asked.

"He's one of the good guys, but...I just can't keep throwing myself at him."

"Sounds like you need to let your inner bad girl loose. I don't think this idiot has seen all there is to Sienna Rossi."

She watched Clare attacking the last half of the climb. She needed to talk to the girl about improving her upper body strength. But she turned Hemi's words over in her head. There were things she wanted to explore. She *did* have an inner bad girl. And Theron definitely hadn't seen all of her. Hell, *she* hadn't seen all of her. Just thinking about what he'd told her he liked left her curious and excited.

Maybe she could do both. Maybe she could be herself, and play a little dirty with Theron.

Once the kids were back on the ground, they gave them a few more pointers and finished the training. Sienna waved goodbye to Hemi and hurried to her quarters. She grabbed a few things before heading to the Enclave kitchen.

As she entered, she nodded to a few of the staff. They were used to her using a little corner of the kitchen. She'd made herself at home in the Blue Mountain Base kitchen and had no problem doing the same at the Enclave. The small cooking unit in her quarters wasn't powerful enough for most of the meals she liked to cook. She repaid them by leaving some extra pizza bases and sauces in the fridges.

She banged around collecting the ingredients she needed and clicking the oven on. She made a mean Italian-style pizza. A family recipe passed down through her mama's family.

"What are you doing here?" a loud voice boomed.

Sienna spun and faced down the big, dark-skinned man bearing down on her. Chef had run the kitchen at Blue Mountain Base. Her gaze skated over the empty left sleeve of his shirt that was tucked up near his shoulder. He'd been injured in their escape from the mountains and was still grieving from the loss of his boyfriend. The wide easy smile was gone but she was pleased to see him finding a place in the Enclave kitchen.

Sienna quickly rolled out the pizza dough. "Pretty sure that's obvious, Chef."

He made a grunting sound. "Our food not good enough?"

"Your food is divine, but as my nonna used to say *prendere per la gola*."

Chef gave her a long look. "I don't speak eye-talian, girl."

"It means to grab someone by the throat, but the closest English saying is the way to a man's heart is through his stomach."

Chef's dark eyes warmed. "Someone caught your eye."

"Someone who is a stubborn idiot." Sienna pulled out the hottest, spiciest salami they had, and when Chef saw it, he graced her with one of his smiles.

"Well, good luck, then."

"Thanks."

"I meant him, girl." Without another word, Chef stomped off, bellowing at someone else across the kitchen.

She made her tomato sauce and found fresh basil that she knew had come from the Garden—an area open to the sun at the top of the escarpment. After she was done, she popped the pizza into the oven, and leaned back against the cupboards.

Something about cooking soothed her. She'd learned to cook by her mama's side, and from her nonna, too. Neither of them could understand why, when she was so good at it, that she didn't want to make a life of it. They'd been even more bemused when she'd joined the Coalition Army. Just one of those contradictions again. No one seemed to truly understand her.

Everyone else in the kitchen was busy, so she pulled out the pretty stationery she'd snagged from her room. Cam had given it to her as a gift. It was pink, and covered in white cherry blossoms. Sienna had spent some time putting some of her perfume on it so it smelled like lilies.

She picked up her favorite pen, thought of Theron, and started writing.

***

Theron's knuckles were bleeding under his tape, but he ignored the pain and kept hitting the punching bag suspended from the ceiling in his quarters. It was the first thing he'd put in when they'd moved to the Enclave. Sweat poured down his face and chest. He'd been at it for an hour and a half. He was *not* going to think of her.

Or how she looked, touching herself. Or the little noises she made when she came.

Fuck. He hit the bag harder. Soon, his lungs were burning as he pushed himself close to his very limits. He'd always loved boxing. His dad had been into it, and had taught him. While the two of them had been beating each other up, his mom had been a runner. He still remembered her coming home from a run, cheeks flushed, a smile on her face. He wished he could just remember her like that, and not as a burnt, black corpse. He walloped the bag again, reveling in the pain and the way it served as a distraction. Boxing had always been an escape for him.

But he was finding no escape today.

Once again, he heard Sienna's breathy cries in his ears.

Fucking hell. He slammed his shoulder against the bag, and set it swinging. He mopped his face with a towel, then dropped to the ground and started doing push-ups, air sawing out of him as he did. He wondered what his parents would have thought of Sienna. He snorted. He already knew they would have taken one look at her and loved her.

His arms were burning when the smell of pizza hit him.

Theron paused, chest touching the floor, and glanced at his door. Only one person made pizza that smelled that good. Then he spotted a slip of paper that had been shoved under his door.

Getting up, he strode over and yanked open the door. The hallway was deserted. Fighting back a shot of disappointment, he spied a pizza box on the ground. With a frown, he leaned down and snatched up both the folded piece of paper and the pizza. He dropped the box on his kitchen counter top and flipped it open. Salami, basil and cheese— his favorite. She always kept it simple.

He lifted the piece of paper up, and instantly the scent of it hit him. *Sienna.* He grabbed a slice of pizza and bit into it. Heat exploded. Damn, it was spicy.

He stared at the loopy writing on the paper and read.

Theron,

My mama always used to tell me il meglio ricolga il peggio. That means bad is the best choice. She told me that I'd understand one day, and now I do.

I hope you enjoy the pizza. I made it extra hot and spicy, which is just how I like my pizza. I know everyone likes to say I'm sweet, but that's only one part of me.

I think of you. Not only your fierce determination when we head into a fight, or the time I know you spend teaching the Enclave kids to box, or the quiet, watchful, and steady core you have.

I have this fantasy of us in a darkened room. You have both of my wrists tied behind my back and you force me to my knees in front of you. You take out that big cock of yours and you tell me to get it hard. Tell me to suck it.

I love it. I love your deep voice and I love watching your reaction when I suck you deep. I love seeing how I make you feel.

I wanted you to know that there are parts of me I want to explore and delve into. Parts I need a man, the right man, to help me explore.

Sienna

He dropped the pizza back in the box, the spice still burning his lips. *Dammit to hell.* But the stinging in his mouth was nothing compared to the images now burned into his brain.

Theron turned, pressing his hands to the back of his neck. His skin felt hot and tight. He stripped off his workout gear and stood there, naked, arms at his sides as he waited for the ventilation to cool him off.

He had to get Sienna out of his head, and he didn't know how.

But his blood was pumping thickly, making his cock rock hard. He dropped onto the bed. It was far too easy to imagine Sienna kneeling between his legs, just as she'd described. Those glorious curls of hers spilling around her bare shoulders. Her wrists tied at the sweet curve of her lower back. Her lips stretching wide as he fed her his cock.

With a groan, he dropped his hand down, stroking himself.

A new memory popped into his head. Of the Christmas party, when he'd come back to his room and stroked himself while thinking of her.

Now, he knew she'd been watching him from the door. Now, he knew that her panties would have been wet, her breathing coming hard and fast as she watched him.

Theron's orgasm ripped through him, and he groaned as he came.

He flopped back on the bed. He didn't feel any better or more relaxed. The orgasm had barely taken the edge off.

There was only one thing that could make him feel better. One woman.

His comm unit pinged, and, his jaw tight, he thumped his fist against it. "What?"

"We have intel on the *oura*," Roth said. "Our mission is a go."

Chapter Eight

Sienna stepped into the Enclave Command Center, ignoring the buzz of comms officers at their comps and people bustling around the room. It didn't matter what time of day it was, it was always busy in here.

She shouldered her way into one of the conference rooms, and spotted her squad.

Her gaze went straight to Theron. He was sprawled in a chair, watching information fill the screens at the front. Then he turned his head, steady hazel eyes meeting hers.

That all-too-familiar, warm sensation filled her belly. Oh yeah, he'd gotten her pizza and note. She shot him a small smile, and then turned her attention to the displays.

As she sat in a chair across from him, she wondered if he'd read every word. If he'd flicked open his trousers and stroked himself...like she had when she'd finished writing it.

"The drone operators have identified the tower in the city where the *oura* is being worked on."

Roth's voice snapped Sienna out of her fantasy. She cleared her throat. Time to focus on the mission.

Arden stepped forward, her elegant face serious. "Golden light was detected coming from this building." A drone image of the shattered ruins of Sydney filled the screen. A still-intact skyscraper rose up in the center.

It was a tall sucker.

"Winton Tower," Mac said.

Arden nodded. "It was a new building. Only just completed the year before the invasion."

"Where was the light spotted?" Theron asked.

Arden's nose wrinkled. "Top floor."

Sienna shook her head. The top floor. Of course. The aliens never made anything easy for them.

"We only spotted a glimmer," Arden said. "We've lost two drones trying to get in close to the buildings, and the drone team won't risk getting closer."

"Lost them?" Roth asked. "How?"

"We don't know," Arden answered. "This area of the city appears to be crawling with raptors. They have increased patrols, and we have confirmed raptors entering and exiting this building with increased frequency." She spread her hands out. "So, we don't have any more information than that. All I can tell you is that the aliens are definitely protecting something inside this building."

"We've been approved for a recon mission," Roth said.

Sienna leaned forward. "We aren't going into the building? To destroy the *oura*?"

"We don't even know for certain if it is an *oura*." A muscle ticked in Roth's jaw. "I will not have another repeat of our mission to the mountains. This could be another trap. We strictly get more intel. Once we know what the hell is going on in that building, then we can decide if we go in." His ice-blue gaze touched each one of them. "Let's get to the Darkswifts."

She saw Theron stay to talk with Roth, and as she shuffled out, Cam bumped her hip against Sienna's. "Nice day for a fly."

Sienna smiled. Nice day to be locked into a very tight space with the man who was driving her crazy.

But she was going to do her best to drive him crazy right back.

She hurried to their locker room, slipped another note into Theron's locker, then dressed at lightspeed.

After she'd checked her newly issued carbine, Sienna made her way to the Darkswift hangar. The sleek, powered, two-man gliders sat neatly all in a row, black hulls gleaming under the lights. Their canopies were retracted, showing a perfect view of the molded seats, where two people could lie down side by side on their stomachs. The craft had dual controls, and ran on a small, silent, thermonuclear engine.

When Theron arrived, she was doing the preflight checks on their craft. She felt a rush of nerves and instantly tamped them down.

When he spotted her, something rippled briefly across his face before it disappeared. "Ready?"

Typical man and typical Theron. He clearly

didn't want to talk.

"Did you get the pizza?"

"The one that nearly singed off my tongue?"

She smiled sweetly and climbed into the Darkswift. "I hope that wasn't all that got singed," she muttered under her breath. She looked over her shoulder, and saw he was staring at her butt.

There was that look again. That dark look that made her shiver. The fantasy she'd scrawled on the note she'd stuck in his locker slammed into her. She imagined those big hands of his digging into her buttocks, followed by the stinging slap of his palm on her skin.

She hissed out a breath. When his hazel gaze met hers, his hands curling into fists by his side, she knew he'd read it.

She lay down on her stomach, settling into her seat.

"Sienna." He towered over her, standing beside the Darkswift.

His disgruntled tone made her want to grin. "Yes?"

"Stop with the notes. I've already told you, nothing can happen between us."

She pictured him as a rock, and her with a hardhat, chipping away at him with a hammer. God, she hoped she wasn't old and gray by the time she wore him down. "We have a mission, Theron. Let's just focus on that for now."

He stared at her, like he was trying to see inside her head, then gave a nod. He circled around to climb into his seat. The Darkswifts weren't designed for men six-and-a-half feet tall, and she smiled as he wedged himself in.

"Got enough room there, Big T?"

He grunted. "Joke never gets old."

For a second, it felt like old times. Before desire and need had twisted them up. "You look like a man who can handle lodging himself into tight spaces very well."

His head jerked up, his gaze burning. "I thought we were focusing on the mission."

She touched the controls, fighting a small smile. "I am." She kept her voice as innocent as possible.

But soon the others arrived, and before she knew it, the canopy was closing, and Theron was firing up the engine.

"Darkswift hangar door opening," Arden's voice came through the comm line.

The Darkswift hangar was located partway up the escarpment. Sienna watched the door open, allowing them a stunning view down into the valley. Arden's calm voice started counting down to take off.

Roth and Mac's Darkswift shot out of the hangar. Next was Cam and Taylor. And then it was their turn.

There was a *thunk* as the launching mechanism released, and then they were flying out through the hangar door.

Theron took the controls, and they headed north toward the city.

Sienna checked the display. "Illusion system up and functioning correctly."

Theron quietly confirmed her assessment. The illusion system made them virtually invisible. Blurring them on visual, masking any sound the craft made, and scattering their location on scans.

It wasn't long before they were flying over the outer suburbs of Sydney. She glanced down through the canopy, staring at the destruction. In some places, the buildings, houses, and shops almost looked untouched, except for overgrown lawns and parks. But in other places, buildings were destroyed, houses burned out, and cars overturned.

There had been so much panic and chaos the night of the invasion. Alien ships appearing in the skies and raining down terror. She'd been on leave from the base and she knew that was the only reason she'd survived. Just east of them, the alien mothership was parked on the remnants of Sydney Airport, and was a hub of operations for the Gizzida in Australia.

"City coming into view," Theron said quietly.

The ragged city skyline filled the horizon. Some buildings were still standing, others half destroyed. Beyond them, arching out over the harbor like some sort of broken skeleton, were the shattered ruins of the Harbor Bridge.

As always, Sienna felt the anger, sadness, and heartache form a small knot in her throat. She thought of her own family, those moments filled with terror, as the aliens bombed the humans from above. All the people who'd died, their lives destroyed.

And those who'd survived—broken and scarred—in the chaos.

She glanced at Theron. She could never let herself forget that they were alive. She'd always tried to live her life to the fullest, to never get trapped doing things she didn't love. The alien invasion hadn't changed that. If anything, it had made that vow more important.

She had a chance for something special with Theron. She was sure of it. Something that so many people no longer had the opportunity to experience.

"*La speranza è l' ultima a morire.*"

"Another of your mother's sayings?" Theron asked.

"Hope is the last thing to die."

He grunted, and she turned her attention back to the tower that they were approaching. "Can you get us closer?"

"Working on it. Don't want to let the raptors know we're here."

She scanned the sky. Even though she couldn't see the other Darkswifts, she knew her squad was close by.

Theron dipped them in lower, and they zoomed closer to the tower. He turned their craft on its side, flying between two buildings.

Sienna saw the Winton building ahead. The *N* had fallen off the sign at the top, leaving it to read *Winto*. Her gaze dropped to the ground and she frowned. "Look."

Theron growled, a scowl crossing his face. "Base

of the tower is heavily fortified."

Sienna murmured her acknowledgment. There were heavy-duty raptor attack vehicles in soul-sucking black, all with turrets mounted on the back, surrounding the building. Raptor patrols marched everywhere. "There are raptors all over the place. You getting shots of all this?" There was a camera mounted below the Darkswift.

"Yes."

She couldn't see a way into the tower anywhere. All the windows were blocked from the inside, and the ground-level entrances were all heavily barricaded. The aliens were protecting this building with everything they had. What the hell was inside?

Theron turned them in a circle and they flew upward, twisting around the tower. Then Sienna spotted something.

"Look! There are some windows open near the top of the tower."

He flew them in closer. Most of the windows had been blacked out, but there were a couple where it looked like the covering was torn, or missing.

"I can see something inside." She peered through the canopy, squinting. "It looks like gold light!"

Suddenly, the Darkswift jerked to a bone-jarring stop, as though they'd hit a wall, head-on.

Sienna was thrown against her harness and her body jerked forward. Her forehead cracked against the console, and pain exploded through her head.

She blinked. The Darkswift sat completely still, hanging near-vertical in midair. *What the hell?*

"Theron?"

"We're stuck on something," he ground out.

She saw his head was arched back and he was staring through the canopy. She followed his gaze and saw something that looked like a near-invisible web.

They weren't stuck *on* something, they were stuck *in* something.

"Theron? Sienna?" Arden's tense voice. "What's happening? You've stopped moving?"

"They have some sort of...web around the building," he said.

Damn. Now that they were up close and stuck, Sienna could see the faint glimmer of the web in the sunlight. This had to be some other kind of defense mechanism the aliens had invented. To capture drones and other aircraft.

The controls beeped and when Theron saw the readout, he cursed. "The web's affecting our illusion system. It isn't functioning."

Oh, no. That meant that Sienna and Theron were stuck in this web, like a bug waiting for a spider to eat them.

***

Theron muttered some curses and revved the Darkswift's engines. The craft rocked wildly, but didn't break free. They were really stuck.

"Roth? We're stuck in some sort of web that's been strung around the building," Theron said across the comm line. "Don't come any closer."

"Acknowledged." Then Roth cursed. "We have pteros incoming."

Great. Just what they needed. The fast alien ships could blow them up with one shot.

"Uh-oh, we have other problems." Sienna pointed out the canopy toward the tower.

Theron followed her movement and saw raptors smashing out windows on the floor ahead of them. *Fuck.* They'd been spotted. Desperately, he tried the engine again, pushing as hard as he could.

Nothing.

Two dark shapes whizzed past them. He caught the distinctive outlines of the pteros. The craft were named for their similarities to pteranodons, with fixed wings and pointed back ends.

He had to get Sienna out of here.

"We need to cut the Darkswift free of the web." Sienna unbuckled her belt.

"What are you doing?" Panic was like acid in his lungs. "Keep your harness on."

She ignored him, and pressed the button to retract the canopy. It started to open.

"I need to cut us free." She tossed her ponytail over her shoulder. "You keep your hands on the controls. Once we're free, we'll drop fast."

Theron knew she was a good climber, but they were stuck several stories above the ground, with no definite handholds and no safety lines. If she fell...

He wanted to leap up and grab her. He wanted to wrap his arms around her and keep her safe.

Gritting his teeth, he forced himself to keep his

hands on the controls and watch as she climbed out of the cockpit and onto the wing of the Darkswift. She moved carefully, but each rock of the Darkswift was dangerous.

Theron's hands flexed on the controls, but he kept his gaze glued to her. *Come on, Sienna. Come on.*

She reached up and touched the barely visible web. She pushed against it. "It's organic," she called back. "A lot like a spider's web. Sticky and strong."

Then, with her other hand, she yanked out her combat knife from the sheath on her thigh and started slicing at the strands.

She kept going, working around the craft. The Darkswift lurched suddenly, dropping slightly to one side. As it did, he saw Sienna clamp onto the wing. His heart goddamn leaped into his throat.

Once he'd adjusted the controls, and the craft had resettled, she moved over, climbing back in his direction. She crossed in front of him, stepping over, her butt dangerously close to his face.

"Sorry."

"Why do I get the feeling you're not sorry?" he grumbled.

She shot him a quick grin, then went to work cutting the web on the other side of the Darkswift.

Suddenly, raptor poison splattered to their left, sizzling as it hit the web. They rocked again and then, nearby, something exploded, raining debris down on them. He cursed and felt the Darkswift tilt. He heard Sienna gasp, and she slid partway down the wing.

"Sienna." He was yanking at his harness.

"I'm okay." She came to a stop, her arms and legs clamped on the wing. She blew out a breath. "I'm almost there. Just a bit more of the web to cut off, and we'll be free."

Theron fought the need to pull her back into the cockpit. He carefully settled back onto his belly and set the Darkswift's laser cannon to sweep across the building where the raptors were firing from. Then he watched as she kept hacking at the last of the web. There were only a few more strands left.

She turned her head, her brown eyes meeting his. "Ready?"

He nodded. "You cut it and hold on. Then get back in here as quickly as you can."

"If I had a free hand, I'd salute," she said dryly. She hacked through the last of the web.

The Darkswift dropped rapidly. They were *free*.

Theron worked the controls, fighting for control. Sienna screamed. He managed to level off the Darkswift, and glanced up. He saw her slip down the wing, and over the side.

His chest froze. His heart stopped. His life stopped.

No! "Sienna. Fuck, Sienna."

He jammed the controls on to auto-hover and launched himself out of the cockpit. The Darkswift rocked wildly, and was moving slowly ahead. She'd fallen. He'd lost her. *She'd fallen.* Holding his breath, he leaned over the edge of the wing, terrified at what he might see.

But she was there, gripping the edge of the wing, legs kicking beneath her. *Thank God.* He grabbed her wrists. With one hard yank, he pulled her slight weight back up.

With an arm around her, he crawled back toward the cockpit. Once they were safely inside, he hit the button to retract the canopy.

She fell into her seat, panting. Theron didn't think. He reached out and grabbed her. He tangled his fingers in her hair, and yanked her in for a quick kiss. Then he dropped her back into her seat, and settled at the controls.

He touched the console, and they shot forward, darting between two decimated skyscrapers.

"Illusion system is back up," Sienna cried.

In his ear, he heard Roth ordering them out of the area. He fell in behind the other Darkswifts as they raced away from the city, evading the pteros.

Sienna laughed. "That was close, but we made it."

"Yeah." He thought his voice sounded calm and controlled.

But in his head, the image of Sienna slipping over the edge of the Darkswift was playing in an endless loop. Inside him, his gut was rolling.

Chapter Nine

After they'd safely landed in the hangar back at the Enclave, Theron thumped the button to retract the canopy. Inside, he was struggling for some control.

Sienna jumped out of the Darkswift, smiling. She reached up and pulled the tie out of her hair, letting her curls fall around her shoulders.

"That was close," she said.

Theron felt the muscles in his jaw work. He couldn't find any words. His fingers curled into his palms.

Next to them, he saw Roth climbing out of his Darkswift. "Nice work, you two. You guys were sitting ducks there for a while."

"Close call," Mac added.

"The raptors aren't stupid. They're clearly coming up with ways to bring down the Darkswifts and drones," Sienna said. "That net—" she shook her head "—genius."

"Yeah." Roth was eyeing Theron's face.

"Theron did some fancy flying," Sienna added.

"Arden's downloading the images we collected," Roth said. "She and the tech team will analyze everything. Then we'll make a plan to get into that tower and take down whatever the hell those alien bastards are doing in there." Roth looked at them all. "Freshen up. Get some rest. Remember that Hell Squad have invited us to a barbecue in the Garden this evening."

"Baby Kari's welcome party," Cam said. "God, that kid is cute."

Theron watched the others walk ahead of him. Cam threw an arm around Sienna's shoulders, both women laughing. They were all coming down off the mission high.

He stomped back to his room. Inside, he tore off his armor and paced his room. He was mad. He couldn't laugh or relax. All he could see was Sienna slipping over the edge of the Darkswift.

For a long, sickening moment, he'd thought he'd lost her.

He'd thought that all the sweetness and light that was Sienna had been extinguished. And yes, the sexy naughtiness he was only just starting to glimpse in her.

He turned to his punching bag and started hammering his fists into it. He'd work off this feeling, bleed off the darkness rising up to choke him.

But even after his knuckles tore and bled, the sensation was still riding him hard. He headed for the shower and kept it cold. Afterward, he pulled on some well-worn jeans and a gray T-shirt. The anger and other emotions were reaching a boiling point and they needed a target.

He knew just who was to blame.

He yanked open his door, and stomped down the

hall. She had no right to risk herself like that. No right to send his pulse rate through the roof and make him worry.

Her room was only a few doors down from his. He lifted a fist and banged.

A second later, she opened the door and stood there, dark hair damp, wearing a blue robe.

"Theron?"

He pushed inside, slamming the door behind him. He crossed her room and put his hands on the back of his neck.

"What's wrong?" she asked.

He spun. "What's wrong? You nearly killed yourself!"

She watched him steadily. "I did my job."

He'd seen her take calculated risks before, but seeing her go over the edge... "You were gone." He heard his voice crack on the last word.

Sienna's face softened and she reached out a hand. "Hey." She stroked his arm. "I'm here. I'm okay."

A vibration went through him, and her touch burned his skin.

He leaned down until his forehead pressed against hers. "Sienna. Seeing you fall...I can't get it out of my head."

"Shh." Her arms wrapped around him.

Holding her, breathing her in, helped settle the seething emotions in him, but it didn't make them go away. Her robe gaped a little, and he had a perfect view of plump, perfectly shaped breasts.

"I can't get you out of my head. You're under my

skin, in my veins."

She went still. "I'm not sorry about that."

"I want you out." He slid his hands up her sides, shaping her rib cage. Sometimes he forgot how small she was. He felt the beat of her heart under his hands. Alive. So damn alive.

She licked her lips. "It doesn't always work like that."

He pulled her into his chest, yanking her up on her toes. He saw desire burning in her gaze. "I need to get you out of my system."

"Oh? And how do you plan to do that?" Her gaze dropped to his lips. "What do you want, Theron?"

He looked down at her. "I want you." The words were torn from him.

She released a long breath. "Just for now? One time?"

His gut was hard as a rock. "I made a vow a long time ago not to get involved long term. I come from bad blood—"

She snorted. "Bullshit. You come from two loving parents."

Theron felt the last of that leash unravel and slip away. He slid a hand into her hair, tangling his fingers in the damp strands. "Once won't be enough."

She smiled. "Good."

He backed toward her bed and sat down. "Get on my lap."

Theron saw her breath hitch, but she climbed on to straddle him. He slid his hands into the mass of her hair and tugged. The desire running through him had turned molten hot.

"If anything I do scares you, you tell me."

"It won't." Her voice was breathy.

"You *tell* me." He traced a finger over her full lips. "You call out *basil* if you want me to stop."

"I don't—"

"I like rough, Sienna, but I don't want to hurt you. I'd kill myself before I did that."

"Okay."

She shifted against him and he pressed his mouth to hers. He took his time kissing her, thorough and deliberate, until she was squirming in his lap. Damn, she tasted so good and kissed him back so eagerly.

"What do you like, Sienna?"

"I don't know. I want to find out."

Fuck. Desire was riding him hard. "Take the robe off."

She lifted her hands, and with a shrug and a push, the robe spilled off her body. She had soft curves, toned legs, and breasts that were just a little too large for her frame. With a groan, he pulled her forward and sucked her nipple into his mouth.

"Oh." Her hands clamped on his head.

He nipped, sucked, and licked until her nipple was hard on his tongue, and she was writhing against him. He slid his mouth to her other breast, enjoying her moans. He sucked hard and she gasped, pulling on his hair.

He smoothed a hand down her belly, feeling her muscles contract. He reached the dark curls between her legs and ran a knuckle through her damp folds.

"That wet all for me, Sienna?" he said against the smooth skin of her breast.

"Yes. Yes."

He slid his finger into her folds and bit her breast, hard enough to make her jerk and cry out. Damn, she was so tight. "You have a sweet, innocent face, but a hot, greedy body, don't you?" He started fingering her slick little clit.

She gasped, hips moving as she rode his hand. "Don't stop, Theron."

He knew she was skating close to the edge and she was liking it. "I give the orders, naughty girl." He pulled his hand away.

She made a protesting cry, her wide brown eyes meeting his.

He cupped her jaw, tilting her head. "Get on your knees, Sienna."

***

Sienna quivered. She was so turned on by Theron's rough, raspy command. She was burning up.

She slid off his powerful thighs and knelt between his legs. She looked up at him and his face set in hard, unsmiling lines. His hazel eyes glittered.

"Take me out."

Eagerly, she tore at the fastening of his jeans. He wasn't wearing any underwear. She stared, her breath hitching again. He was so big.

"Touch it." His voice sounded like gravel.

She circled his cock, running her hand over the silken hardness of him. She saw his body jerk and loved his reaction. She wasn't the only one lost in the need.

"What else?" she whispered.

"You know what else. Suck it, naughty girl." His big hand slipped into her hair, pulling her head gently to the side to give himself the perfect view.

Sienna leaned forward and sucked the big head of his cock inside her mouth.

She was fascinated with the shape and feel of him. The swollen head, the interesting ridges, the hardness. There was one thick vein running down the underside of his cock and she licked it, following it with her tongue. Then she moved back and sucked him back in.

She took more of him, forcing herself to relax. The way his big body trembled, the muscles in his thighs clenching, made her even hotter. She couldn't wait to drive him over the edge and taste all of him.

"Goddammit," he ground out. "You love it, don't you? You love having my big cock in your greedy mouth."

She sucked him harder and moaned around his cock.

Suddenly, he pulled her off him and yanked her up.

"No," she cried.

"Be quiet." He lay her back on the bed, his hand diving between her legs. His fingers filled her and her hips bucked upward. "There's my naughty girl. You like it?"

"Yes," she panted.

"This is mine now. Later, I'm going to lick you here." He thumbed her clit and Sienna saw bright blotches of light explode in her vision.

"I'm going to suck this pretty little clit. I'm going to make you come over and over again."

"No." It sounded like the best torture. "More."

"Which is it, Sienna?"

"More. I'm hurting, Theron."

He climbed over her, his big, hard body covering hers. He nudged her legs apart, yanking one of her thighs around his waist. She felt his cock butt against her hot folds.

Then he stopped, and she thought she'd lose her mind.

"Your contraceptive implant still functioning?"

"Yes."

"Beg me," he growled.

"Please, Theron."

"Please what?"

"Come inside me. Please, I want your cock inside me."

"Not good enough." He slapped her hip, hard enough to sting.

"Fuck me, Theron. Now!"

With a growl, he thrust into her, his thickness stretching her. "Oh, I'm going to fuck you, naughty girl."

He grabbed her hands and yanked them above her head, pushing them into the bed. And then his hips started thrusting, his cock sliding in and out of her. He was so big, his penetration so all-consuming.

"Fuck, you are so tight and hot, Sienna." His words were almost unrecognizable.

The sensations flooding her were driving her out of her mind. She bucked her hips up against him, trying to get more of him.

"Stay still." He thrust into her harder, rougher than before.

Excitement coursed through her. She saw the control in his eyes, felt his strength. He was stronger than her, and that turned her on. He kept her pinned down, and that turned her on, too. His full lips, usually set in a straight line, curled with a harsh edge.

"Mine," he growled. "To fuck as I please. Your mouth and pussy are mine."

Excitement spiked, and she felt her body winding tighter. "No." She made a few breathy, helpless sounds. The role-play ratcheted up her desire. "Let me go."

"Hell no, naughty girl. I can't wait to come inside you and shoot deep."

Her breathless cries were punctuated by the slap of his flesh against hers as he thrust inside of her, deep and powerful. His breathing was harsh, perspiration covering them. She pushed against his wrists, gratified when his thrusts increased.

She felt her orgasm looming, bigger and stronger than ever before. "Theron."

"That's it, Sienna." He slid one hand between

their straining bodies, and she felt his finger graze her clit. She jerked and cried out. "Time for you to come all over my big cock."

He tweaked her swollen clit again, and she just shattered. She felt tossed by a giant wave, and came with a sharp snap. He hammered into her now.

"Say my name," he ordered. "Say it."

"Theron!" She threw her head back.

He grunted, and she felt his body go tense. She watched his face as his release hit. Suddenly, he pulled out of her, and with two rough jerks, he came all over her belly.

"Fucking hell." He dropped down onto the bed beside her and yanked her back against his side. She felt the rapid rise and fall of his chest.

She couldn't move. Hell, didn't *want* to move. She felt well-used, sexy as hell, and surrounded. Safe. She turned her head to look at his face. It had lost the hard edge, and looked surprisingly relaxed. She ran her tongue over her teeth feeling pretty pleased with herself. "So, did you get me out from under your skin?"

A sound vibrated through his chest. His fingers tangled in her hair, stroking. "Hmm, not sure. Thinking something still isn't quite right." Hazel eyes met hers, his fingers tracing down her cheekbone. "Think we'll have to do it again."

He sounded relaxed and content. That made her happy. "You weren't...as rough as I'd imagined."

Theron pressed a kiss to her shoulder. "I was taking it easy."

She froze. "You weren't yourself?" She rolled over onto her belly. "You held back—?"

"Hey." His hands slid down her side, curving possessively over her hip and buttock. "Sienna, I fucking loved it. I loved touching you, hearing the noises you made, the way your tight body clutched my cock."

"But you weren't—"

He gripped her chin. "I'm teasing you. I'm not a damn monster. You saw me get off. It's covering your belly."

She wrinkled her nose, her panic easing, and gave a little smirk. "Actually, it's smeared all over my bed covers."

"I'll clean up the mess." He climbed off the bed and headed into her bathroom.

Sienna rolled onto her back. When Theron returned, he was holding a washcloth. He stroked the cloth over her skin, cleaning her off. Her heart clenched.

"Theron, I don't want you to hold back next time." She wanted him to find some new pieces of herself.

Something flared in his gaze. He reared up, flipped her onto her belly and pushed her into the covers. She tried to move but he held her down with a big hand in the middle of her back.

She felt him looming behind her. His lips grazed her spine, his stubble scraping over her skin. He moved upward and by the time his lips brushed her ear, she was writhing. Slow and thorough. That was Theron.

"Don't move." A dark growl.

She couldn't help herself, she giggled. He nipped her ear and she giggled again.

Suddenly, she felt his palm crack against her ass. She gasped, the shock and sting taking her by surprise. His hand smoothed over her cheek.

"Keep it up, naughty girl, and I'll fuck you harder than you ever have been before."

Chapter Ten

Sienna struggled beneath him.

God, Theron loved holding her down, seeing how soft she looked compared to his strong hands. He slapped her ass again, and she tried to hide her moan in the covers.

"You like this, don't you?"

"No," she cried, but she was lifting her ass up to his palm.

He spanked her again and again. Between the sharp cracks of his palm, he caressed her, sliding his hands down her thighs and between her legs.

"You lying to me, naughty girl?" He growled the words, running his fingers through her wet folds. "You're soaking wet."

"No."

"Yes." He teased her. "Your clit is swollen."

She got into the spirit of their play, wrestling against him. "Stop."

He spanked her again, liking the pinkness of her ass cheeks. "You want this. You want me to force you?" He slid his hand between her thighs again. She parted her legs, pushing back, her breath coming in sharp pants. "Oh, yeah, my naughty girl likes it."

"No, stop."

"Shut up."

"Stop, please." She struggled again.

He leaned down, nipping at her shoulder, then her earlobe. "Keep struggling. It makes me harder." He pressed against her, the dampness of his cock rubbing over the skin of her ass. "I can't wait to take you, put my big cock in and shoot inside you."

He grabbed her hips and yanked her up to her knees. He nudged her thighs apart with one of his own, then, without warning her, he slid inside her.

Sienna let out a long moan. God, she was so tight and hot. He started driving into her, brutal unforgiving thrusts.

"Say my name," he demanded.

"No," she choked out, even as she shoved her ass back against him.

He slid a hand into her hair, fisting it in her curls, and forcing her head back. Damn, desire was stamped on her face and she was lost in it. He slowed down, fucking her deep and thoroughly.

With each thrust, he heard her whimper.

"God...move," she begged.

"Say. My. Name."

"Theron. Please, move faster, Theron."

He did, starting to lose his rhythm as his release grew in his body like a growling, hungry beast. He knew she was riding the edge, about to come. He slapped her ass one more time, and felt her explode. Her back arched and she screamed.

Theron pounded into her a few more times before he thrust deep and finished inside her.

He collapsed down beside Sienna, an arm and leg thrown over her prone body. What the hell had that been? Sure, it had been a while since he'd had sex, but he'd had some pretty varied and creative sex in his time.

No one had pushed him to the edge like his sweet Sienna, though. He looked at her and saw she'd pressed her cheek into the covers. Her eyes were closed, and she was panting.

He swallowed. Was she regretting it? Had he been too rough? He gripped her chin, pulling her face his way. "Okay?"

She smiled at him, her eyes opening, her gaze a little bit dazed and unfocused. "Better than okay. I...do you think you can be a little rougher next time?"

He sucked in a breath. God, she was perfect. He'd thought she wouldn't want him like this, but she'd matched him step for step. "Sienna."

She giggled now. "I loved when you spanked me. No one's ever done that before. When you were fucking me, I could feel the scrape of your skin on my sensitive ass. And when you pulled my hair..." She nibbled on her lip.

He cupped her jaw. "Tell me."

"The sting was only slight, but it made me more aroused."

Hell. Some emotion bloomed in him. One he didn't recognize, but made him feel damn good. One that pushed back the darkness he usually struggled with.

"We should get a bit of rest," he told her.

"Oh." She looked disappointed.

He tugged her closer, settling on the bed. "Even I need a bit of a break before I can fuck you again."

She snuggled into him. "Okay. How do you like to sleep, Big T? Spooning? On your own side?"

"Don't know."

She lifted her head. "What do you mean?"

"Never shared my bed with a woman. I...usually leave after the fun's over."

Her brown eyes flickered. "Do you want to go?"

He yanked her so she sprawled against his chest. "Nope."

She settled into him and Theron decided he could spend every night drifting off to sleep to the sound of Sienna's quiet breathing.

***

Sienna woke up balanced precariously on the edge of the bed.

Theron wasn't lying when he said he'd never shared a bed. He was taking up the entire thing. The only thing stopping her from tumbling to the floor was the hard band of Theron's arm around her waist.

She heard a soft beeping from somewhere in the room. She remembered that he'd set an alarm, so they wouldn't miss the barbecue. That was after he'd finished fucking her on the table. She licked her lips. He'd pressed her down on the surface and kept her hands clasped in the small of her back while he'd taken her. Almost like she'd been tied up.

And she'd loved every second.

"Hey, Big T, time to get ready for the party." She nudged him and heard him grunt.

She slipped out from under his arm and headed for the bathroom. She was more than a little sore, but she loved it. From the ache between her legs to the slight burn on her backside.

After a quick shower, she stepped out and watched him shaving with her razor, only a white towel around his hips. She let her eyes linger on the muscles in his back.

"You keep looking at me like that—" his gaze met hers in the mirror "—we won't just be late, we'll miss the party entirely."

"We can't miss it. They'll be waiting for us." She made a shooing motion. "Go, get dressed and I'll meet you in the hall."

He turned, took a step in her direction. She went damp, wondering what other magical, sexy, and dirty things he could do to her.

He cursed under his breath. "See you in five minutes."

"I need fifteen." She set her hands on her hips. "I'm a woman."

His gaze drifted down her towel-clad body. "Yes, you are." When his eyes met hers, the gold in them looked molten-hot. "After the party..."

The suggestion hung there, taut, and hot. She nodded, her voice breathy. "After the party."

Once he'd left, she rummaged through her

closet. She yanked on some pretty blue underwear. She needed something pretty, but secretly sexy. She paused, smiling. Theron was *hers*. Her smile widened.

She pulled out a white dress with a cinched-in waist, a fuller skirt that hit just above her knees, and thin straps. It was simple, with a neckline that dipped enough to give a hint of cleavage, and the color was a perfect contrast with her dusky skin. She swiped on a tiny bit of makeup, left her hair out in a mass of curls, and spritzed on her favorite perfume.

Sienna twirled in front of her mirror. *Not bad.*

Theron was leaning against the wall in the corridor. "Ready?"

She closed her door. "Ready." Heat bloomed inside her. That seemed to happen whenever she looked at him. It didn't matter if he was wearing his armor or casual clothes. He'd pulled on well-worn jeans that hugged his mighty-fine ass and legs, and a navy-blue cotton shirt that stretched over his broad chest. He was mouthwatering, and all hers.

His gaze raked over her as he pushed away from the wall. He fingered the thin strap of her dress. "Pretty."

Where his fingers brushed against her, her skin tingled. "Thanks."

All of a sudden, he dropped down on one knee, his face level with her belly. Her breath hitched.

"What are—?"

He circled one of her ankles and slid his hands

up her leg—calf, knee, thigh. The desire that slammed into her was shocking. Anyone could walk into the corridor and see them. How could she feel this much again, so soon? The man had spent several hours inside her, and had made her orgasm so many times she'd lost count.

His fingers brushed her inner thigh, and then across the satin of her panties. He looked up at her, hooking one finger in the elastic. "I want these."

Sienna knew it wasn't a request. Her belly fluttering like it was filled with butterflies, she let him slide her panties down her legs. She pressed a hand to his shoulder, as he helped her step out of them. He stood, brought the panties up, stroking the silky fabric for a second before he stuck them in the pocket of his jeans.

"Now we're ready to go," he told her.

They headed down the corridor. She'd always known that there was more to Theron, something a little darker. But over the last year and a half, she'd never guessed at the sexy man beneath his tough, solid façade.

They reached a tunnel where the small carriages that led up the escarpment to the Garden waited. They settled in, side-by-side, and the autonomous vehicle moved along the tunnel, heading upward.

The tunnel was dark, lit at intervals by soft lights on the wall. There were signs of the original purpose of the tunnels here—pipes strung along the roof, patches of dark coal in the wall.

A second later, a big hand started bunching up the skirt of her dress, and Sienna closed her eyes.

His hand stroked her thigh again, and then he wasted no time sliding a finger through her curls.

"I want to know you're wet for me while we're at the party." His voice was deep. "So wet that it's making your thighs sticky."

So dirty. She licked her lips and let her legs fall apart.

He rubbed her clit before sliding a thick finger inside her. He worked it in and out, before sliding in a second one. She controlled a gasp. Theron had very big hands.

Then, she felt the vehicle slow, and his fingers slid out of her. Her eyes popped open, and she made a small cry to protest the loss of him. She felt empty, wanting.

He was smiling at her. "We're here." He smoothed her dress down.

Ahead was the door leading into the Garden. Sienna composed herself as best she could, and prayed her legs would hold her. Walking beside Theron, the two of them entered the Garden. And damn the man, her thighs were sticky.

The Garden never failed to make her smile. The large bowl had been cut into the escarpment overlooking the Enclave. Rock walls rose up, and overhead, she saw the faint glint of sunset lighting the sky. All around were gardens, lush grass, and trees. Fresh fruits and vegetables were grown in fenced-off gardens. A children's play area sat beneath the taller trees, which were strung with fairy lights.

It was one of the best parts of the Enclave, and

actually quite safe. Sienna knew the open top was protected by an illusion system, and retractable doors could be closed, if required.

She heard muffled conversation and laughter—the deeper tones of the men, and Cam's distinctive, melodic chuckle. They were all clustered around the picnic tables under the trees. Someone had covered one tree in pink bows.

In the center of the crowd stood Cruz Ramos—second in command of Hell Squad—along with his partner, Santha. Santha was sitting in a comfortable chair, while Cruz had their newborn daughter tucked into the crook of his arm. He looked like he'd been doing it for years.

He was talking with Hell Squad's leader, Marcus, and Roth. Marcus was sipping a beer, one arm around his wife, Elle. The rest of Hell Squad and their partners, as well as the members of Squad Nine, were dotted around the space, sitting, standing, plucking food off the loaded trays on the table.

"Hey, leave some for the rest of us." Hell Squad's only female soldier, Claudia, slapped the man beside her in the back of his head.

Hell Squad's sniper spun around, frowning. "I'm hungry, Frost."

"So is everyone else, Baird."

"You are so ornery," he muttered. Then he fisted a hand in her shirt and yanked her against him. "Only one way I know to sweeten your disposition." He slammed his mouth down on hers.

Sienna gave Claudia credit; she fought against

the onslaught for a good three seconds, before she gave in. The tough female soldier melted, wrapping her arms around her partner.

They were a perfect example of a couple who loved and worked together. As she and Theron joined the group, she saw Hemi look up from his chair. His gaze swiveled between her and Theron, his brows rising. Then he winked at her.

Okay, it couldn't be that obvious that she and Theron had gotten naked together. She was sure no one else would notice.

Suddenly, Cam leaped off the picnic table she was sitting on. "Oh, you did *not!*"

Sienna stiffened, surprised that Theron seemed so relaxed beside her.

"Cam," Sienna said in a warning tone.

Taylor and Mac flanked their friend, the women staring at them.

"They did," Mac said.

Taylor shook her head. "Dammit. Devlin picked it at the Christmas party, and I didn't believe him. I mean it's Theron...and Sienna." She glanced at her man, a former spy and one of the Enclave's best on the intel team. "Guess I lost our bet."

A smile crossed Devlin's handsome face, and it told them all just how he'd extract his winnings from Taylor.

Sienna's face was burning. Of course, her friends would make a big deal of it. "Look, we—"

"Banged each other's brains out," Theron said. "Numerous times. Planning to do it again." His gaze met Roth's. "A lot."

Sienna's mouth dropped open. "Theron!"

"I'm not lying or hiding us."

She struggled through feeling happy, embarrassed, and horrified. She decided to go with happy.

He grabbed her hand and pulled her toward the table. "Let's eat." His gaze lingered on her face. "I'm starving."

As Theron piled food on a plate, Sienna gave Santha and Cruz a warm smile. "Your baby girl is getting bigger every day."

Santha looked like she was trying not to burst out laughing. "She is. And luckily for us, she's a great baby."

Sienna looked around. "Where's Bryony?" She didn't see their adopted daughter—a girl Cruz and Santha had rescued from an alien lab—anywhere. The girl was usually hovering over her new sister.

"Sleepover," Cruz said, lifting the baby up for a snuggle. "Only time I get my smallest girl to myself."

Sienna felt her ovaries sigh. There was something about a sexy tough guy with a swirl of tattoos on his muscled arm snuggling a baby.

As the conversation shifted, she sensed Roth move up beside her. She glanced at her friend and boss, suddenly nervous about what he might say. She knew the old rules of the Coalition military didn't apply in this new world of theirs, but he would be completely within his rights to have concerns.

"Roth—"

"Just remember, no alcohol. We could still get called up for the *oura* mission."

She thought she caught a faint hint of concern in his gaze, but he was smiling.

Sienna relaxed when Theron returned, and took the soda and the plate he offered. Soon, they were sitting amongst their friends, eating and drinking.

"Any luck on the data we collected in the city?" Theron asked.

A frown crossed Roth's rugged face. "Nothing yet. They're working around the clock, and the tech team is in chaos, trying to work out what this alien web is and those alien pods."

Sienna listened to the conversations around her. She watched Hemi staring at Cam with covetous eyes. Cam was pretending to ignore him. Her friend had defenses that would make a castle proud. Hemi had his work cut out for him, but the man was stubborn and determined.

"Hemi, where's the rest of your squad?" Sienna asked.

"On their way." He sipped his homebrewed beer. "They want to challenge the Hell Squad pussies to a rugby match."

There was a chorus of pithy replies from Hell Squad, Shaw's the loudest.

"Hey, baby present." Cruz covered a sleeping Kari's tiny ears.

Sienna chuckled, and glanced over at Theron, who was listening to something Roth was saying. As she nibbled on her food, she felt his leg brush against hers. He wasn't looking at her, but she knew he was aware of her. She heard Taylor laugh, and saw her friend staring up at Devlin, love glowing off them. They'd survived hellish raptor captivity and escaped together. The two of them were perfect for each other.

Sienna was reminded that this was her family now. She knew she'd always have that dull pain in her chest when she thought of her of mama, her sisters, her nonna, and her family. Maybe she'd always feel that tiny pinch of guilt that she'd not only survived, but that she felt such happiness being with her squad. She'd fought alongside these people every day for almost two years. Trusted them with her life. They'd forged bonds in battle that went beyond blood.

For the first time in her life, she felt truly accepted. Her squad accepted her as she was, and those dark and dirty moments with Theron had made other things click into place for her, too. *Si*, her mama would have welcomed Theron with open arms, and a huge plate of spaghetti.

"Holy hell, the testosterone level in here just skyrocketed," Roth's partner, Avery, breathed. Sienna saw the woman looking back toward the door, and swiveled to take her own look.

Oh, boy. Avery was not wrong.

The rest of the berserkers had arrived.

Squad Three was made up of the kind of men mothers warned their daughters to steer well clear of. These weren't bad boys, these were deadly men—former bikers, ex-cons, and mercenaries.

Tane stalked in, dreadlocks loose around his

compelling face. She'd never seen him smile, but the look suited him. He moved like some sort of predator on the hunt. His squad members surrounded him.

Tall, handsome Ash Connors, with two sleeves of colorful tattoos on his muscular arms. His best friend, Levi King, was beside him. Levi was a couple of inches shorter than his friend, but no less muscular, and with plenty of tattoos of his own. His long, brown hair was pulled back in a messy knot at the back of his head, and he was sporting a sexy-looking goatee. The men had run a motorcycle club before the invasion.

On Tane's other side was Griff Callan—a former cop and ex-con. He wore his hair a little shaggy, and it was a deep, oak brown. He had the hard look of a man who'd done time in a Coalition supermax prison for murder. Two steps behind him was the man Sienna considered the most dangerous of the berserkers—hell, maybe the entire Enclave.

Unlike the other berserkers, he was dressed in slacks and a white shirt. Dominic Santora had dark, Italian good looks, but his brown eyes were almost black, and held a deadly stillness that always gave her shivers. No one talked about where Dom was from, or what he'd done before the invasion...but Sienna had her suspicions.

Hemi stood, knocking his knuckles against Tane's. Soon, the berserkers were all nursing drinks and sprawling in chairs.

Cam nudged some things aside on the table to make room. A few of the kitchen staff appeared, setting down desserts.

"I bribed some of the kitchen staff for special treats." Cam winked at Sienna, and pointed to bowls of chocolate and vanilla ice cream.

Sienna wrinkled her nose. "I finished the last of my favorite sprinkles. Need to ask Squad Eight to keep an eye out for more on their next raid."

She was addicted to the sweet things. Luckily for her, Squad Eight was made up of non-military fighters who were usually tasked with raids to collect goods like foodstuffs, clothing, and medicine.

Theron reached into his pocket and pulled something out. He held it up to her. "For you."

Frowning, she took the paper-wrapped jar. She ripped the covering off, and her heart clenched.

"I knew your stash was running low," he said.

Theron had given her a new jar of the sugary sprinkles she loved. "Where—?"

A shrug of his big shoulder. "They're handmade. I traded a few boxing lessons for the son of a lady in the kitchen who made them for me."

With her heart full, she reached out and touched his arm. "Thanks, Big T."

He cupped her chin, one hand falling to her thigh beneath the table. When he stroked dangerously close to her inner thigh, her pulse tripped.

Suddenly, Hemi stood and whistled. He flicked a smirk at Shaw. "So, Hell Squad ready to get their asses handed to them on the rugby field?"

There was a chorus of good-natured catcalls and insults. Tane moved onto an open patch of grass, spinning a rugby ball in his hands.

Hemi slapped Theron on the shoulder. "Need you and Roth to referee."

The men moved off to the grassy area, and almost as one, yanked their shirts over their heads, displaying an impressive show of muscles and ink.

Cam sank down beside Sienna, licking at her ice cream cone, her eyes glued to the man-candy spectacle. "Oh, this is going to be good."

Sienna watched Theron organizing the teams, blind to all the prime specimens of masculinity. Well, okay, almost blind. But her gaze lingered most on Theron.

In that peaceful, almost completely normal moment, there was no alien apocalypse, no death or suffering, no dangerous missions. He glanced her way and smiled.

Something unfurled inside her and her chest hitched. *Uh oh.* She had a feeling this sensation was how it felt to take the first step toward falling in love.

Chapter Eleven

Sienna led Theron back to her room, happiness bubbling inside her. She felt good. They'd had a great time at the barbecue with their friends. The berserkers had managed to just squeak in for a win in the rugby match, but not before they'd all suffered a few bruises and one suspected broken nose.

She glanced up at Theron, his big body moving with his usual powerful stride. She loved being with him...and despite all the goodness, how much she wanted him left her a little terrified.

At her door, she pressed her palm to the lock, disengaging the latch. He crowded in behind her, spinning her, his mouth crashing down on hers. The kiss instantly turned wild, their tongues tangling, her hands clutching at his shoulders. He ran a hand under her skirt, sliding his fingers inside her before she could protest. She moaned.

"Let me get the lights," she panted. She wanted to see his rugged face.

"Leave the lights off." He pulled away from her and stepped back. "Just turn on the bathroom light."

She bit her lip, walking on wobbly legs to the

bathroom. She loved that bossy, gravelly tone. And she knew that later, it would take on a rougher edge she found exciting.

She flicked on the bathroom light. It gave a subdued glow into the main room of her quarters. Almost romantic.

She turned. "Do you—?"

Theron wasn't where he'd been standing. Frowning, she took a few steps, glancing around. She couldn't see him.

"Theron?"

Suddenly, she was grabbed roughly from behind. A hand slammed over her mouth, and she stifled a startled scream.

"Don't fight or I'll hurt you." His breath was hot on her cheek.

His hard body was plastered against her back. She felt his hard cock digging into her lower back. His hand was rough as it slid down her body. He bunched her skirt in his hand, before he shoved it up to expose her bare bottom.

Sienna's pulse raced. Excitement rushed through her, and she felt a rush of dampness between her thighs.

His hand palmed her buttock. "Nice." He swung her around and pushed her up against the wall. "Press your hands flat against the wall." A deep growl.

She jerked against him, trying to break free.

"No, you don't." He used his strength to subdue her struggles. "I'm going to fuck you, lady. Hard. Nothing you can do about it."

Sienna struggled harder, desire swamping her. She tried to bite his palm.

"Uh-uh." His fingers dug into her skin. "I'm fucking you, lady. So hard you'll be crying about how deep I go. Now, hands on the wall."

She pressed her palms against the cool wall. Behind her, she felt his hot hand running along the length of her ass. She arched her back, trying to hold back her moans. He smacked her buttock, the sweet sting zinging through her. A small moan escaped. "No. Let me go."

"Be quiet." Another stinging slap to her other cheek, then she heard the rasp of a zipper and his clothes shifting.

Then without warning, his thighs brushed against her sensitive buttocks, and he rammed his thick cock inside her.

His bellow mingled with Sienna's sharp scream.

He reared back and thrust back in. He found a punishing rhythm that had her stretched to the limit.

"Oh, God. I can't..." Her feet lifted off the ground, forcing her up on her toes. Even if aliens invaded the base right at this very moment, there was no way she would stop. He was so rough, so dominating and forceful.

"You should see this pretty picture," he growled. "Me pumping into you and your sweet ass jiggling with each impact."

"More," she panted.

"Hold on then, naughty girl."

***

Fuck. Theron gripped Sienna's hips, pounding inside her.

She was clawing at the wall, begging him for more. He pulled out, enjoying her dismayed cry.

He nudged her toward the closest surface, her table. He pushed her hips against the edge and bent her over it. He forced her face down until her cheek was pressed against the smooth wood. He got behind her, pressing a hand down on her back, and thrust back inside her.

Hot and tight, she made him forget everything, made him feel like an animal in a mating frenzy. She was slamming her ass back against him, desperate for more. All he could do was feel.

He reached under her, flicking at her swollen clit. She let out a strangled cry, her body clamping on his cock like a vise. He felt every muscle in his body tightening, and the driving need to possess her, own her, ravaged him. He hated that she still had an implant, hated even a chemical barrier between them.

He gripped one of her legs and forced her knee up on the table. It changed his angle of penetration, and gave him perfect access. He drove back into her, thrusting against her like a wild man. He saw her hands move to grip the edge of the table, her knuckles turning white.

"Take my come, Sienna. Push your ass back at me and take it all."

She did, and then she shattered. Her scream,

followed by the sob of his name, was too much. He pressed his body over her, their slick skin sticking together. He sank his teeth into her shoulder as he thrust one last time and poured himself inside her with a harsh groan.

He collapsed on her, pinning her to the table. "Fucking hell, Sienna."

One of her sweet giggles. "That was so hot."

He tucked his face into the curve of her neck and breathed her in.

"Give me a chance to recover and then we'll go again."

"Again?" She turned her head to look at him, licking her lips. "I'd like that."

He just stared at her. He didn't want to move or leave the room. He wanted to keep Sienna in here, naked, all to himself. His to touch, caress, and love. Hell, how could he have been such an idiot to think that sweet Sienna, with her hidden spine of steel, couldn't handle him?

Love? The word made his muscles tense. What the hell did the son of a drug-addicted prostitute know about love?

"Theron."

He focused on Sienna and touched his lips to hers, gentle this time. Which was strange. He didn't do gentle. But as she sighed into his mouth and the slow, searching kiss continued, he decided that there was something to be said for taking your time, for savoring and exploring.

She shifted against him, a sexy little shimmy. Then her teeth sank into his bottom lip.

He slid a hand down and cupped her ass. "Such a sexy little tease, aren't you? Wearing sexy clothes for me, shaking that ass at me, writing me sexy notes."

She smiled at him. Suddenly, there was a thumping on the door. Sienna squeaked, trying to wriggle out from under him.

"It's Roth." Roth's disembodied voice from the other side of the door. "You weren't answering my call." Their leader's voice was dry as dust.

Call? Theron glanced at the comm unit beside the bed. He hadn't heard anything except Sienna's cries and the thump of his heart.

He stood and helped Sienna do the same. She wobbled a little as she pushed her dress down.

"We're here," she called back. "What's going on?"

"They've finished analyzing the intel from the city," Roth told them. "They've confirmed that a giant *oura* is in the top of Winton Tower. Squad Nine is heading back into the city to destroy it."

"We're on our way." Theron jerked his jeans back on. He watched Sienna head for her wardrobe, stripping her dress off.

His playful, sexy lover was gone, and in her place was the soldier he respected. The woman he trusted with his life.

Soon, they were in their gear and meeting with Roth in the Command Center. General Holmes was there, looking grim-faced. On the screen was an image of Winton Tower, captured by the Darkswifts.

"We got the footage enhanced enough to confirm

that there is a giant *oura* at the top of Winton Tower." The general's blue gaze swept across them all. "Large enough to control any survivors in the city."

Not good. Theron crossed his arms over his chest.

"We've also had some disturbing reports from other survivor bases around the globe," Holmes said. "They are reporting large *oura* in their areas, too."

"So the Gizzida lure all the remaining human survivors out, and then what?" Theron asked.

"Use their secret weapon," Sienna said.

Holmes ran a hand through his hair. "That's our best guess. The problem is, we don't know what this weapon does. Destroying the *oura* is the mission priority this time." He turned to Roth. "But if you find any intel on this secret weapon, you bring it back."

"Acknowledged," Roth answered.

"The raptor defense web is still in place around the tower," Holmes said. "We haven't come up with a way to neutralize it. That means we can't risk you taking Darkswifts or Hawks in."

"So, we'll get dropped off close by and walk the rest of the way," Roth suggested.

Arden swiveled to face them. Their comms officer was seated in front of a comp. "The drone team is reporting sightings of this web in other parts of the city."

The news was like a punch to Theron's gut. "We can't fly in?"

Roth's jaw was tight. "We'll drive in. In the Z6-Hunters."

Holmes clasped his hands behind his back. "The area around the city is clogged with barricades and obstacles. Looks like the raptors have been blocking the streets and access roads to prevent that."

"But you have a plan?" Sienna asked.

Holmes nodded, and turned his gaze to the back of the room. Theron turned, and watched Tane and Hemi stride in, already armored up. The only difference was, the berserkers didn't cover their arms, which left their black ink on display.

Tane nodded at Squad Nine. "Everybody up for a little motorcycle ride?"

Theron's brows rose. "We're going to ride in?"

Holmes nodded. "Squad Three has been outfitting bikes for missions like this. They're maneuverable, and all have thermonuclear engines."

"I've seen their bikes," Theron said. "They were not quiet."

Tane's lips moved in what might have been a brief smile. "Not those bikes. These ones we've especially designed for stealth."

The room fell silent. Theron turned the proposition over in his head. Not a bad idea.

"We'll take you in close," Tane said, "then head off to cause a distraction and keep the heat off you."

Distraction to a berserker meant blowing stuff up, flames, and general chaos.

"The tech team and Reed have put together

several explosive charges for you to take in and use to destroy the *oura* globe," Holmes said.

Reed was Hell Squad's explosives guru, and damn good with anything that went boom.

Sienna was staring at the screen. "If we aren't flying in, that means we need to sneak into the building and fight our way to the top."

Holmes face turned grim again. "Yes."

Shit. Theron knew the building would be riddled with raptors. "And back out again." There was a good chance they wouldn't make it back.

"We've had tougher missions," Roth said. "Noah's team has rigged up some wingsuits for us. Everyone needs to add it to their armor."

"Wingsuits?" Cam said incredulously. "You mean, in case we have to jump off the top of a massive skyscraper?" The woman shuddered. "Nuh uh. I'll take my chances with the raptors."

"Let's hope we won't need them," Roth said dryly. "Noah also said the suits affect the armor's illusion systems. While you're flying, you're fully visible."

"Great," Cam muttered.

Roth looked at them all. "Squad Nine, ready to save the world?"

"Let's do it," Mac said.

Taylor, Cam, and Sienna all nodded.

For the first time in his life, Theron looked at Sienna and terror filled him. His battle calm had vanished. Yes, they'd fought dangerous missions together, too many to count. But before today, he hadn't been inside her, listened to her breathy cries, and heard her scream his name. He hadn't slept beside her, listened to her quiet breathing, and felt her curl into him.

He wouldn't let down his squad. He'd get the job done. But for Theron, his mission priority was keeping Sienna Rossi safe.

***

Sienna felt the motorcycle vibrate beneath her. The huge bike was fitted with all-terrain tires, and a small, thermonuclear engine. She sat right behind Theron, with her arms clasped around his waist.

The rest of her squad were all getting ready, and checking their rides. Beside them, Mac was riding behind Roth, and Cam was riding a third bike with Taylor behind her. Roth was carefully setting the explosive charges into armored storage compartments on the side of his bike.

Sienna had stashed a bag on the back of their bike, too. She'd packed some of her climbing gear, her experimental climbing gloves, and her extra laser pistol. On a mission like this, it paid to be prepared.

Ahead of them, the berserkers sat on their bikes, waiting.

None of their escorts were sharing bikes. Each berserker had his own motorcycle, and each one was heavily modified and outfitted differently. There was a lot of armor plating involved, as well as some missile launchers.

They really were all wild and a little scary.

"Ready?" Tane called out, his face its usual expressionless mask.

Roth nodded. "Let's do this."

Tane nodded, and his bike shot forward. The rest of Squad Three followed him into a tunnel. Roth went next, and then Theron set their bike in motion. They rolled almost silently through the twists and turns of the tunnel, until the road began to ascend.

Soon, they exited through a hidden entrance, and into the afternoon heat.

They bounced across a grassy field, before riding over a downed wire fence and onto a road. Ahead, the berserkers shot off, looking like a big, bad biker gang. They headed north, Arden's calm tones in their earpieces, along with the snarky voice of Squad Three's comms officer. Indiana 'Indy' Bennett was in her late twenties, but didn't let any of the berserkers boss her around. Sienna had heard that the berserkers had been through a number of comms officers, before Indy—a family friend of Griff's—had stuck.

"You follow my directions this time, or I'll lead you right into a nest of rexes," Indy said, her voice sharp.

"Aw, Indy, babe," Hemi drawled. "Chill."

"You don't tell me to chill, Rahia. Last time, you guys ended up having to fight your way out of three raptor patrols. You made me spill my coffee all over my comp. My very expensive and nearly depleted Arabica."

Hemi snorted. "We love you, too."

"Indy." Tane's cool voice.

The young woman sighed. "Don't get yourselves killed out there. I don't need all the single Enclave women sobbing all over me."

Sienna smiled, pressing her cheek to Theron's back. There was no sign of any raptors or other aliens as they entered the outer suburbs of Sydney. Instead of studying the empty schools, abandoned houses, and looted stores as they passed by, she thought of Theron. Of what they'd done back in her room. She shivered. Everything he did to her turned her on, and she was excited to experience more. He *saw* her. He knew her better than anyone had before.

He reached back and patted her thigh. Damn. For the first time ever, she hated her armor. She reminded herself that she needed to focus on the mission. Whatever they faced in the city, she wanted to make sure they made it back safely.

They whizzed around debris and toppled cars and trucks. A few times, they had to go up on the sidewalk, zipping around street lights and rubble and wreckage that had accumulated. Slowly, sadness surged inside her. Sienna hated seeing the ruin up close, the heartbreaking destruction and emptiness. It made her imagine the streets of Rome and where her family had lived. Did they look the same as this?

Her heart clenched, and she wondered if they'd ever beat the Gizzida. The aliens outnumbered them many times over, and humans had been reduced to small pockets of fighters and survivors, scattered across the planet. Her arms tightened around Theron, and she felt him drop one hand from the bike's handlebars onto where hers rested on his hard stomach. He squeezed, like he could read her thoughts.

She looked at the back of his head, then over at Roth, her squad mates, the strong men of Squad Three. The sadness and despair receded a bit. They still had hope. As long as they had each other, and kept fighting, there was still hope.

Soon, she saw the city's skyscrapers rising up on the horizon ahead. A few times, they had to adjust their route to avoid raptor patrols. Finally, Tane pulled his bike to a stop, and raised a hand. They all pulled in around the squad leader.

"Indy says the barricades and patrols get more dense from here." Tane's dark eyes were unreadable. "This is the point where you have to go in by foot."

Mac and Roth climbed off their bike. "Thanks for the escort."

Tane inclined his head. "Destroy that fucking globe and get back to base. I'll buy the first round."

"I want wine," Taylor called out. "The good stuff."

"Screw wine," Cam said. "I want bourbon. Sweet, smooth, and expensive."

A tiny smile tweaked Tane's lips. "That can be arranged." He glanced at his brother—Hemi was watching Cam, his jaw tight—before looking back at them. "Get back to the Enclave in one piece."

Cam lifted her carbine up to her shoulder. "Don't

you worry your pretty little heads about us."

Sienna climbed off the bike and grabbed her small pack. She hitched it over her shoulder, and gripped her carbine.

Roth, Theron, and Taylor stashed the bikes in an abandoned building. The squad would come back for them later. Then, they watched the berserkers speed off down the street.

"Let's go," Roth said. "Armor illusion systems on, and keep it quiet."

Sienna watched as each member of her squad flickered and disappeared, blurred by the illusion systems that were now built into their armor.

They moved in formation, Mac in the lead, and Theron bringing up the rear. They didn't need to talk in order to move together with a precision they'd honed over the last year and a half.

They hadn't gone far when Mac's voice whispered over the comm line. "Raptors coming in from the east."

"Inside," Roth ordered.

Chapter Twelve

They all hurried off the street and into a building that looked like it had once been an office. Sienna crouched beside Theron, behind a long reception desk in the lobby.

Overhead, ceiling panels and wires hung down. Chairs had been overturned, and leaves and trash had collected in piles, blown in through the broken windows and open door.

She heard the raptors approach, the clomp of their heavy boots and their distinctive guttural voices growing louder. She peeked around the corner of the desk, just as a raptor stomped past.

"Arden says there are raptor patrols on every street," Roth murmured quietly. "We'll have to move slowly and carefully."

Once the street was clear, they slipped out of the building and continued their journey. As they got closer to the tower, the raptor patrols became more numerous, and more frequent. Multiple times, they stood stock-still in doorways, or ducked through buildings to avoid detection.

They closed in on the Winton Tower. Sienna

arched her head back, staring up at the skyscraper. The building speared into the sky, mostly intact, except for some shattered windows. She wondered just what the hell the aliens were doing on the top floor, besides housing the *oura*.

Roth hunkered down behind an overturned van, and they all crouched beside him, so close together, that they were all inside each other's illusions. Roth pulled out his binocs, and was studying the scene ahead of them.

He cursed quietly. "Dammit. The base of the tower is even more heavily fortified than on our last trip. I can't see a way in."

Even without binocs, Sienna could see the raptors had piled up cars, vans, and blocks of concrete to create a barricade around the tower. Armed raptors were everywhere.

Suddenly, a boom sounded, and the ground beneath them shook. They turned to look behind them. Several blocks away, a cloud of smoke was rising in the air.

Several patrols of raptors started shouting and running toward the explosion.

Score one for the berserkers. As her squad debated options, Sienna studied the area. Across the street was another office tower that was almost as tall as the Winton. Something had crashed through the side of it, leaving a giant hole torn into its side, but it was miraculously still standing.

She glanced between the two towers. The barricade didn't extend around the second building. "I have an idea."

The others went quiet, all of them looking at her.

"What?" Roth asked.

She pointed at the second building. "We can use that building, instead."

Roth frowned. "I'm listening."

"I'll climb up the outside of the building. I brought my climbing gear, and I have a zip line. I can zip across to the Winton and—"

"What?" Theron was vibrating with tension. "That's insane. No."

A cold sensation brushed over her skin. Theron knew her skills. "It's a good—"

"No."

"I can do this. You guys can run interference down here, and with my illusion armor, no one will even notice me. It's far less risky than trying to infiltrate the building from the bottom."

"Unless you fucking fall," Theron bit out. "You'll be exposed."

"My illusion system will keep me hidden."

"We've seen it fail before. Taylor almost died!"

The cold had expanded, lodging in her gut. God, he wasn't going to turn into an idiot like every other man in her life, was he? "Don't you think I can do this?"

A muscle worked in his jaw. "It's a bad idea. Crazy. You can't climb up slick glass."

"I can with these." She whipped the climbing gloves out of her bag. "You've seen them in action."

He shook his head. "No. Just no."

"I'm the best climber in the squad." *Please*

believe in me, Theron. Pain drove into her heart. Now that they'd slept together, maybe things had changed. Maybe he only saw the lover, and not the rest of her.

Theron stared at her, his face granite hard. Stubborn as always. He looked back at Roth. "We're wasting time. We need a real plan."

Her heart twisted. Just like every other man in her life, he couldn't accept her as she was. She sucked in a breath, pushing the sorrow away. She couldn't deal with this now. It would have to wait until later. She looked back at Roth, feeling Theron's glare boring into her. "I can do this."

Roth gave one vicious shake of his head. "You both need to put your personal stuff aside." He looked at the building. "Sienna, you're our best climber, and we have to do whatever we can to destroy the *oura* up there." He pulled out a black bag, which held the explosive charges. "Go. Climb the building."

A burst of relief hit her. She took the bag, swinging it onto her back. At least Roth trusted her. "I'm on it."

Theron looked like his jaw was going to break under the strain of gritting his teeth. "Fine. But I'm going with her."

To protect her? Because he didn't think she could do the job? "I *can* do this—"

"I know you can," he ground out. "But once you get into the Winton, you can't take on all the raptors up there alone. You need backup, and that's me."

She stared at him, something trembling inside her. She pulled out her second pair of climbing gloves and slapped them against his chest.

Roth nodded. "Okay. Both of you, go. Good luck, and we'll see you on the other side."

Cam slapped Sienna on the back, while Taylor winked and Mac nodded. As the others slipped away, Sienna faced the building they had to climb. Anger and hurt churned inside her, but she blocked them out of her head. She couldn't worry about her and Theron right now.

When the way was clear, the two of them raced across the street, running to the side of the building. They paused there, and pulled on their climbing gloves.

"Let's move down that alleyway," she said. It would get them off the street, and give them some cover.

He nodded and they slipped down the narrow gap. Once, it had probably been a shortcut for city workers slipping out of the office for coffee or lunch. Now, it was filled with rotting trash and debris, and against one wall, she spotted the skeletal remains of a body.

An orange glow emanating from the other side of a dumpster caught her eye. She skirted it, and felt something squelch under her boot.

"What the hell?" she muttered.

Theron grabbed her arm and pulled her back. "It's like that pod we saw in the colony outside the Enclave."

It was attached to the side of the building,

pulsing. Tentacles snaked out of it, reaching in all directions.

Sienna wrinkled her nose. "What are these things?"

"Let's avoid it."

She stepped around the alien thing, and faced the building. Close enough that she saw her reflection in the glass. A soldier ready to do what had to be done. She pressed one gloved hand to the glass, and felt her sticky palm suction on.

"Sienna."

She looked up. Theron was inside her illusion and she met his gaze in the glass. Her heart clenched. "Let's get this done."

"I just wanted to keep you safe."

She closed her eyes. "I don't need your protection."

"I..." He muttered a curse. "That's what drives me crazy."

It would happen again. Men just couldn't seem to help it with her. "We'll talk later. We have a job to do."

He pressed up behind her, his hand circling the nape of her neck. "Sienna, I told you I'm not easy or nice. I knew I'd screw up...I'm sorry."

She told herself not to soften, even as his touch sent tingles down her spine. "I'll expect a better grovel than that."

His fingers brushed her skin, and she could sense that he was about to say more, but from outside the alley, shouts and carbine fire sounded. Their squad had engaged.

"Let's get moving." She pressed her second hand to the glass, took a deep breath, and started upward.

She had gone a few meters and looked down. She saw the blur that told her Theron was moving upward, slowly and steadily. Down below, she saw something explode and heard both alien weapons and carbine fire. She said a silent prayer for her squad and then focused on climbing.

As they moved higher, the wind picked up, tearing at the tie holding her hair in a ponytail. Theron brushed close to her, moving inside her illusion. She saw his face set in hard lines. He was looking grimly at the glass and not looking down.

Sienna glanced down and her stomach did a slow turn. She wasn't afraid of heights, but damn, they were a long way up, and they still had a fair distance to go.

They continued to climb, until they reached a floor where most of the windows were smashed. She peered through the opening, into what looked like a high-end apartment. She gasped. The place was filled with dozens of the same orange glowing pods—on the floor, the walls and the ceilings. Spreading tentacles were approaching the edges of the broken windows, as though they were going to start curling along the outside of the tower.

She didn't like the look of this at all.

"Keep going." Theron's voice slipped up to her on the wind.

With a nod, Sienna turned away from the broken glass and the ugly alien pods inside. She

155

skirted around to an unbroken window and kept climbing.

***

Don't do it. Theron told himself not to do it.

He looked down.

Fuck. He wasn't phobic, but looking at the ground so far below them made him a little dizzy.

Grimly, he followed Sienna, just putting one hand in front of the other. He hoped to hell the geek squad hadn't screwed up with these gecko gloves.

He knew he'd messed up down below. He'd made Sienna think he was like every other asshole she'd been with. How could she believe he didn't see her, all of her? He blew out a breath. *Because you acted like one of the assholes.*

Damn, it was hard to watch your woman walk— or climb—into danger. But he knew in order to win back her trust, he had to rein it in.

They passed another broken window, and Theron glanced inside at the open-plan office. Smashed comps littered the floor, and scraps of paper flapped in the breeze. The place was riddled with more of the alien pods and tendrils.

He stared at the closest one. As he watched, he saw something move inside the pod. They had to find out what the hell these things were, but now wasn't the time. He forced his gaze away, and kept going.

Finally, Sienna signaled to him. "I think we're

high enough." She was looking over to the Winton Tower. They looked to be a few stories below the top.

She reached over her shoulder and pulled out the compact zip line launcher.

"Hold me," she said.

He kept one hand stuck to the glass, and wrapped his other arm around her waist. He steadied her, as she aimed the launcher toward the neighboring tower.

The zip line whizzed across the space and thumped into the other building. Sienna swiveled and clamped the unit onto the glass above their heads. She reached up and tested the line.

"I'll go first," Theron told her.

She skewered him with a sharp look. "This is my mission—"

He pulled her close. "I'm sorry for my caveman instinct of wanting to keep you safe. It isn't because I fucking think you're a princess or aren't capable. You are one of the most capable women I know."

"Theron, we're dangling off the side of a building."

"You are one of the few people I trust to have my back—in a fight, at a party, anywhere."

Her breath hitched. "Damn you, I was going to make you grovel."

"I will. Later." He brushed her jaw with his thumb. "I'm your squad mate, your friend, and now also the man who had his cock inside you. I want, no, I *need* to do something to protect you, even though I know you can protect yourself. It's in my bones."

She sniffed. "I think it's in your testosterone."

"Probably. I know you hate it when everyone looks at you and sees your pretty face, but I see you, Sienna. And I like everything about you. I see the soldier and I see the woman. A woman who will always fight for what's right, who loves her friends, who can laugh in the middle of an apocalypse."

"Damn you." Her face softened. "Okay, you can go first."

"Just like that?" he said, surprised.

She smiled at him. "You explained. You didn't just go all alpha male caveman, and demand and grunt."

Theron wanted to kiss her. "I probably will screw up sometimes, and the caveman will make the odd appearance."

"And I will ensure you regret it when you do."

God, she was gorgeous. Helpless to resist, he leaned down and pressed a quick kiss to her lips. "Let's destroy an alien mind-control globe, and then get home."

Theron reached up and clipped the dangling line from the zip line to his belt. He took a deep breath, and cast one more glance back at Sienna.

"See you on the other side, Big T."

He nodded and pressed the release button.

He zoomed out over the open space, the street far below. He reminded himself that he was invisible. When he looked back toward the building, he could no longer see Sienna.

Don't look down. He turned to fix his gaze on the Winton Tower.

But suddenly, halfway across, he started to slow. His momentum died, and he came to a stop, hanging in the middle of the zip line. *Fuck.*

"Hang on, Theron." Sienna's voice through his earpiece. "I'm checking the zip line mechanism."

He blew out a breath. She'd get it sorted out. He looked at the Winton building. Through some of the upper windows, he saw raptors moving about. God, if one looked out and noticed the zip line, he was screwed.

The seconds ticked by, feeling like minutes. Then, he started moving again. *Thank God.* Sienna had gotten it fixed.

The Winton Tower approached. He jerked to a halt just inches from the glass. He pressed one glove to the window, and then unclipped himself from the zip line. "Made it." He heard a small whine as the line retracted.

He waited impatiently for her, picturing her clipping on.

"On my way," she murmured.

He saw a faint blur in the air, and knew she was zipping across. Nerves chewed at him. Funny how he didn't care so much for himself, but knowing she was out there, exposed above a massive drop, made his gut twist.

But then she flickered into view inside his illusion, and her body bumped into his.

"Are you okay?" she asked.

He nodded. She pressed her palms to the glass

beside him. They climbed up another story toward a broken window. When they reached it, he peered over the edge.

It opened into a stairwell. *Perfect*. He gestured for her to go first, and then he followed her in. They both came up with their carbines raised. He pointed ahead, and they moved toward the stairs. He knew they needed to go up a few more floors to reach the *oura*.

They moved silently, rounded yet another landing, and headed up again. By his calculation, one more level, and they'd have the right floor.

The squeak of a door opening above them, followed by raptor grunts, caught his ear.

Sienna and Theron froze. He looked around. *Dammit*. There was nowhere to hide. They were on the landing in a stairwell, and there were no hiding spots.

He grabbed her and pressed her back against the wall. They stood, still and silent. Theron didn't dare draw a breath. He hoped to hell the illusion systems would hide them well enough.

Two raptors came down the stairs, heavy boots thumping on the concrete floor. They were grunting to each other in their language. They moved past Sienna and Theron, just over a meter away.

Shit. Another centimeter, and they'd be inside the armor's illusion and able to see them.

His pulse pounded. He waited for shouts.

But the next second, the aliens passed by and continued downward. Theron released the air stuck in his lungs. He felt Sienna do the same.

He grabbed her hand and pointed up. She nodded, and together, they continued. They reached the final landing at the top of the stairwell, and found the door ajar. Golden light washed out through the gap.

Sienna nudged him, lifting her goggles from around her neck. They pulled them over their eyes, and then slipped inside the room.

Chapter Thirteen

Sienna kept her back pressed to the wall, scanning their surroundings. The room was dominated by an enormous *oura* globe made of gold glass. Raptors moved around it, engaged in some sort of work that involved the massive thing.

The top floor of the building had once been a restaurant, offering wonderful views of the city and the harbor. Now, most of the tables and chairs had been shoved aside, although some were still in use, covered in black raptor comp screens, and other things Sienna couldn't identify.

On the other side of the room were two swinging double doors, leading into the kitchen. They were guarded by several raptors. She arched her neck, trying to see inside, but could only make out raptor silhouettes.

Theron pointed to some nearby tables and, in a crouch, they raced over and ducked down. As they both studied the *oura,* she pulled out one of the small explosive charges that Reed had given her. Theron did the same.

Then he grabbed her arm, and nodded his head.

The doors to the kitchen opened suddenly, and Sienna got a glimpse of lots of those strange orange pods all over the floor and walls. She grimaced. What the hell were they? But as the doors swung shut with a soft thump, she took a deep breath. Their mission was about destroying the *oura*. That's all she could think about right now.

Together, they crept closer to the *oura*. She ran her fingers over the charge. They needed to get both right onto the globe.

Theron pulled her close, his lips pressed to her ear. "You take the charges and get them set. I'll lay down some carbine fire and cause a distraction." He pressed the second charge into her palm.

She nodded, and turned her head until their lips brushed. "Stay safe."

He deepened the kiss and then pulled back. "You too. You get even a graze, I'll be very unhappy."

She winked at him and took the second charge. *Stay safe, Big T.* She said the words over and over in her head, and drank in his rugged face, just one part of him she was falling hopelessly in love with. Along with his light and dark, his rough and sweet.

Like he'd read her mind, he touched her chin. Then, he turned and hustled over to what looked like it had been the restaurant's bar.

As he lifted his carbine, Sienna forced herself to focus on sneaking closer to the *oura*. Damn, there were far too many raptors crowded around it.

Theron started laying down cover fire.

Raptors ran, ducked, and dived. Sienna crouched, and heard the sound of raptor weapons and the splatter of poison.

Near the *oura*, most of the raptors had dived for

cover. Focusing, Sienna raced toward the globe. She ducked and dodged raptors that were heading toward the mysterious source of the weapons fire.

Suddenly, one slammed into her, stepping inside her illusion. Burning-red eyes widened. It opened its teeth-filled mouth to shout, but she yanked out her combat knife and stabbed him in the stomach. She worked the blade through his thick, scaled skin, and when she yanked it back, the alien fell to the floor groaning.

There were only two tables between her and the *oura*. Sienna dropped to her hands and knees, and crawled under the tables. On the other side, she popped up, careful to keep her gaze averted from the globe. She knew the goggles helped, but if she looked directly at the golden light and got caught...then both she and Theron were dead.

She crouched beside the giant globe. The damn thing was the size of an SUV and the top of it brushed the ceiling. She pressed one charge to the base of the *oura*. She quickly moved to the other side, and pressed the second charge in place.

Done. Ten seconds. She leaped up and ran back toward Theron. Reed had promised the charges would give a small, localized explosion, but she wasn't taking any risks. She and Theron needed to get back to the stairwell and get back to the zip line.

Nine. Raptor poison shot through the air in front of her. She pivoted and raised her carbine. *Eight.* Going down on one knee, she fired at the line of raptors on the other side of the room.

Seven. Sienna dived and landed near a table. She tipped it over and took cover behind it. Theron was still firing. *Six.* More poison came her way and she ducked down, hearing it sizzling through something. *Five.* Damn, she was pinned down.

Four. She popped up again, firing. She saw several raptors running through the doors into the kitchen. *Three.*

"Theron, run!" she shouted. *Two.*

One. The explosion was deafening. The *oura* exploded in a shower of lethal golden glass. As the projectiles shot everywhere, Sienna ducked as low to the ground as she could.

Raptors around her screamed and shouted.

"Sienna?" Theron's panicked voice in her earpiece.

She could barely hear over the ringing in her ears. "I'm okay."

"We need to go."

She popped up and took two steps in his direction. She couldn't see him, but assumed from the trajectory of his fire, he was still near the bar.

The doors to the kitchen banged open. She swiveled.

What. The. Hell?

Sienna stood there, frozen. Several raptors were urging a...creature out of the kitchen and toward the balcony doors.

It towered over the raptors. It had six legs like some mutated insect, but the center of it glowed orange. It had a thick, black exoskeleton, a swollen belly, and an elongated head with a toothless, round mouth that dripped drool. It skittered along with the raptors.

And they were very clearly protecting it.

Theron skidded in beside her. "You okay?"

She nodded. "They're getting away. Theron, whatever the hell that thing is, it's important."

His gaze narrowed on the new alien, and the raptors hurrying it out onto the wide balcony.

"We have to stop them." She gripped his forearm. "This thing could be something to do with the secret weapon."

He glanced back at the stairwell, then muttered a curse. They jogged across the room in pursuit. When they reached the kitchen doors, strange sounds coming from inside reached her ears.

Now what? They paused, and Sienna carefully pushed open one of the doors.

The room was now empty, except for the alien pods. Inside the closest one, she saw a black shadow writhing. Some pods were vibrating.

"Aw, fuck." Theron lifted his weapon. "This can't be good."

They didn't have time for this. "Let's—"

The closest pod exploded, sending orange goo splattering over Sienna and Theron. The stench was horrible.

For a second, she was worried it might be poisonous or corrosive, like most alien substances, but she quickly realized it was just sticky, smelly, and gross.

Something tumbled out of the pod, flopping wetly around on the ground like a fish. Then the creature managed to get up on its shaky legs.

It growled.

It was some sort of hybrid alien dog, like they'd seen in the town near the Enclave. Sienna aimed her carbine, looking into the creature's soulless red eyes.

It growled again and took a step toward them.

Theron fired. The dog let out a wild howl that made Sienna wince. Theron shot it again, and the creature skidded across the floor.

All the other pods were now vibrating together.

"Theron..." Sienna took a step backward.

The pods all simultaneously burst open, splattering goo everywhere. More animals appeared—more dogs, a mutated cat, some large birds—all covered in goo-soaked fur, feathers, and scales.

"Go!" Theron shouted.

They backed out the door, firing, heading toward the balcony.

There was a roar of sound from outside, and through the glass balcony doors, Sienna watched a large alien ship fly past. It wasn't a ptero. It was bigger, boxier in shape. Some sort of cargo ship, she guessed. It was heading straight for their building.

"There's an alien ship incoming," she yelled over their carbine fire and the snarls of the animals. "Looks like it's headed for the roof."

Suddenly, a huge explosion rocked the building. Light flared outside, burning her eyes. Sienna staggered. The glass windows blew out, and Theron's body slammed into hers. He covered her as glass splintered around them. She heard the hybrid animals yipping and screeching in pain.

"Hell, what now?" Theron muttered.

The blast was too big to have been their squad or the berserkers. Sienna nudged Theron back and they got to their feet. She stared out the window, and saw flames and smoke rising up from across the street.

From the building they'd scaled.

"Let's get to the roof," Theron said.

She nodded but when she glanced back out the window, her stomach contracted into a hard knot.

"Theron."

The tone of her voice made him stop and look her way. He followed her gaze.

The building they'd climbed up was falling, teetering over like a tower of blocks kicked over by an irate child.

And it was heading right toward them.

***

Theron grabbed Sienna and yanked her toward the stairwell. It would be more reinforced, and hopefully give them some protection.

He thundered across the room. Just a few more meters...

Boom.

The building shuddered, knocking them off their feet. Dust, plaster, and brick rained down on them. Theron rolled Sienna beneath him, and covered her with his body. He felt something large hit the back of his armor, but he didn't move, until the shower of debris stopped.

Cautiously, he lifted his head. His gut cramped. He looked through a gaping hole in the building just meters away from them. The second building was leaning against Winton Tower at a forty-five-degree angle. Both buildings were rocking. *Fucking hell.*

"Theron." Sienna pushed against him. "Are you okay?"

He nodded, sitting up. When she saw the damage and the toppled building, she gasped.

"Theron? Sienna?" Roth's frantic voice through their earpieces.

"We're all right," Theron answered.

"Raptors blew out the neighboring building. Both are unstable. They are going to come down. Repeat, the buildings will collapse. You need to get out of there."

Grimly, Theron looked at where the stairwell had been. It was now nothing but air.

"We'll work on it," he told Roth.

The other man cursed. "I'm calling in a Hawk. Nets and raptors be damned."

"We have the wingsuits," Sienna said.

Yes, they did. And they both knew they were far too high up to use them safely. If they could get lower, they might work. But lower wasn't an option.

Dammit. He wasn't going to let Sienna die here. He gritted his teeth. The aliens weren't getting her, either. They stood, dusting themselves off.

"We have to go up," he said.

To where the aliens were.

He saw steely resolve solidify in her brown eyes. She lifted her carbine, and nodded. Together, they moved toward the still-intact balcony. He bet that once upon a time, it had been a fancy place to have cocktails and watch the sunset. Now, the wide terrace was littered with debris and overturned tables and chairs.

"There." Sienna pointed to an external staircase leading up to the roof level above. They took the stairs, their boots ringing on the metal.

As they climbed, Theron felt the building rock beneath them. He grabbed the railing to steady himself. "Move it!"

They were both panting as they reached the top and ran out onto the roof. It was flat and empty except for a yellow circle with an *H* painted in the center.

Ahead, raptors grunted and growled, as they loaded the orange-bellied creature into the back of the same large, alien ship. The large transport was hovering right beside the building. The creature reared up, screeching, its two forelegs waving madly. It was clearly not happy with the situation.

"Come on." Theron pulled her across the roof.

The building started to tilt beneath their feet, pushed over by the force of the collapsed second building. They both started to slip and slide on the uneven surface.

Shit. They had nowhere to go. Theron looked at the alien ship. The raptors had forced the creature in and disappeared inside. The ship started to pull away from the tower.

He gripped Sienna and swung her into his arms.

"Theron!" Her shout was snatched away by the wind, and the roar of the ship's engines.

He held her tight against his chest. The wide back door of the ship was still open.

Theron sprinted toward the vessel. Sienna's life depended on him now. Impossibly, he picked up even more speed.

Her hands gripped onto his shoulders.

As they neared the edge of the building, he saw the gap between the roof and the ship widening.

He leaped out into the air.

Time slowed. Theron did the one thing he knew he shouldn't do, and looked down. He got a dizzying glimpse of the street far below. Really far below.

The gaping doorway of the alien ship got closer, wind buffeting them. He stretched out an arm, as though that action could help him reach it.

Then they hit the edge of the ship and rolled inside.

Chapter Fourteen

The alien ship did a wide turn. Sienna and Theron slid across the floor, and she stifled a gasp.

They'd made it.

She scrambled upright. They'd made it, all right. Out of the damn frying pan and into the back of a damn alien ship. Sienna flicked her gaze around the space, relieved to discover they were alone. At least, for the moment. She let out a long, slow breath, and then studied their surroundings more carefully. The walls and floor were a spongy, black, organic substance. Every now and then, a pulse of red light traced through the walls—like neon blood through veins.

Lots of organic cables dangled from the roof, and nearby, strange boxes and crates were stacked high. They were clearly in a storage area of the ship. Attached to the far wall were two large, bony shapes. Sienna had used plenty of different exosuits in the military—from combat versions to cargo units for heavy lifting. These looked like the raptor version. They were made from a bone-like substance, and had sturdy legs and two large arms for lifting.

172

"Sienna? Are you all right?"

She turned around and smacked Theron in the chest. "We are *never* jumping off a skyscraper again. Ever."

He yanked her into his arms, pressing his cheek against hers. "I hope not."

With a shaky sigh, she relaxed into him. Then, a noise from the front of the ship made them both tense. He grabbed her, and pulled her into a corner behind some boxes. She took a few deep breaths, trying to calm her still-racing pulse.

"Roth? Do you copy?" Theron touched his earpiece. "Roth? Arden?"

When Sienna met his gaze, he shook his head.

"If anyone is receiving this, Sienna and I are on an alien ship headed south. I repeat, aboard an alien ship headed south."

The noises in the cargo bay got louder, resolving into raptor voices. Theron fell silent. They needed to trust their illusion armor would keep them hidden, until they could find a way off.

Theron nudged her and pointed. Just ahead of them, a long, narrow window was set into the side of the ship, near floor-level. It was made of a transparent, amber material, with faint black striations through it, but she could see the city below clearly enough.

The landscape was rushing by beneath them, but Sienna spotted a stretch of beach. "We're heading south. Fast."

A loud screech echoed through the cargo bay, raising goose bumps on the back of her neck. They both peered around some crates.

The six-legged creature with the swollen orange belly was chained to a wall, right at the front of the cargo bay. It was sitting down, and looked like it was resting.

"Creepy thing."

"That's a good name for it," Theron said. "A creeper."

"What do you think it is?"

"Yet another ugly-ass, dangerous alien monster."

There was her cheery man. Sienna stared at the creature for a moment, unable to shake the feeling that there was more to this alien than what they'd already seen. She glanced back at the window, and frowned. How the hell were they going to get off the ship without being discovered?

In a blink, they flew over a familiar city, that sat tucked up against the ocean. "We just passed over Wollongong." Which meant they'd just passed the Enclave, too.

"Let's see where we're headed," Theron said. "We might be able to find out more about this creeper, and what they're doing with it."

Sienna nodded. But she was excruciatingly aware that the risk of getting caught during this mission was sky-high. They might never see their squad again. Her heart clenched. Might never get home to the Enclave.

She and Theron were alone.

"Theron?" Her mouth went dry. She traced his strong, tough face with her gaze. A face she knew as well as her own. A man she knew through to his core. Every corner of his soul. "I have something to tell you."

He raised a brow. "Right now? It's not exactly the best time."

She scowled. "Says the man who stopped to grovel whilst hanging off the side of a skyscraper." She grabbed his hand. "We might not get another chance."

His fingers tangled with hers. "Don't say that." A dark growl.

"We could get caught and tortured. Or stuck in a genesis tank and turned into raptors. Or we could crash in a fiery ball of flames—"

He grabbed her, shaking her gently. "I get it. But I won't let any of that happen to you." His tone was fierce.

Something melted inside her. There he was. Her solid, grounded, and fierce protector. How could he ever believe he'd failed his family or friends? "I love you, Theron."

His hazel eyes darkened. "I know."

Sienna waited. And then waited another second. "*You know?* Theron, you aren't some scoundrel space smuggler. You need to say more than that."

He just looked at her.

She let out an exasperated breath. "I pour out my love. I accept you for who you are. I knock some sense into that stubborn head of yours—"

With one hard yank, he toppled her against him. Then his mouth was on hers, forcing her lips apart, his tongue plundering her mouth. His fingers curled around her throat, hard enough to send excitement flaring through her belly.

"I'm no expert in love," he said, his thumb brushing her racing pulse. "I saw that my parents were in love, and after a long time, I learned they loved me. But the time I spent with my birth mother…"

"Blood does not define you, Theron. It's what we do, the choices we make."

"I've made a few bad choices, too. I didn't think I would find love. And I especially didn't think I'd find it in the middle of this fucked-up invasion."

She touched her hand to his stubbled jaw. "Neither did I. But I love you."

His hands tightened on her. "I'm still not sure I deserve you."

"Oh, I know you don't," she said in a teasing tone. "But I love you anyway. You might have a few rough edges, but there's a hero under all that rugged stubbornness."

Raptor voices interrupted their conversation, and Theron pulled her closer to the wall. They huddled quietly as the alien ship raced south. The raptors were checking on the creeper that snapped at them halfheartedly, before lowering its head again.

Then, Sienna felt the kind of rumbles and shakes that indicated the ship's velocity was slowing. She looked up at Theron. He was frowning. The ship tilted slightly, starting its descent. Sienna leaned toward the window, peering out at their surroundings. Mountains. One peak in particular looked familiar.

"That's Mount Kosciusko," she murmured. The tallest mountain in Australia, and part of the Snowy Mountains. Although, to be fair, Kosciusko wasn't very high, and the mountains here weren't very snowy. Where the hell was this ship going?

The ship's vibration changed, and the vessel began to drop more steeply.

Sienna pressed her nose to the window. Ahead, lay a sweeping valley filled with a long lake. In the distance, she saw huge, white pipes snaking up over a hill. She stilled. It was a hydro-electric power station—part of the Snowy Mountain Hydro-electric Scheme. At the base of the pipes was a squat, gray concrete building that housed the turbines for the power generation.

But as the ship turned a little more, her blood turned to ice.

"What is it?" Theron demanded.

She moved aside so he could see. Near the power station, stretching out across the valley, was an army of aliens—pteros, vehicles, raptors in exosuits carrying equipment, raptor patrols. But worse, in the center of the aliens were hundreds of creepers like the one in their ship. They were milling around, among thousands of glowing orange pods.

And it looked like Sienna and Theron's ship was about to land in the middle of it all.

***

Theron stared out the window, his jaw hurting under the strain of his frown. This was *not* good.

177

Aliens as far as he could see. They filled the entire fucking valley.

Shit. If they landed in the middle of this, he and Sienna had no chance of escape. They'd be caught, and...images flooded his head. Imagining his Sienna in the hands of the raptors...

His jaw clenched tighter. *No.* That wasn't going to happen.

"We need to go." He pulled her up.

"Go?" Her eyes widened. "What do you mean, go?"

"We have to jump." He led her over to the door, studying the glowing control panel, and the slashes of the raptor language on it.

Her eyes widened even more. "Jump?"

"We have the wingsuits."

He touched the controls, stabbing randomly at the panel.

Sienna shook her head. "Theron, the wingsuits aren't designed for a jump like this."

"You suggested jumping off a skyscraper earlier! We have to risk it." They needed to get off before the ship reached the aliens. If they could get into the trees, they had a chance.

She muttered a curse. "Fine. My nonna used to say *è meglio cader dalla finestra che dal tetto.*"

The panel kept beeping at Theron. Finally, he yanked his combat knife out and stabbed the controls. Sparks sprayed out. "What's that mean?"

"It's better to fall from a window than from the roof."

"Smart lady." Next, he jammed his blade

between the doors and started to pry them open. When he had enough room, he shoved his hands in and heaved, using all his strength. He managed to open the doors wide enough for them to squeeze through. Air whistled through the gap. He guessed they were still several hundred meters above the ground.

Sienna's face hardened. "I think there—"

Guttural shouts filled the cargo area. Theron heard the thump of boots hitting the floor, and raptors flooded in.

They were out of time. Theron grabbed Sienna's hand and yanked her through the gap and off the ship.

She screamed. As they fell through the air, they tumbled end over end, and her hand slipped out of his. He fought to right himself. *Dammit.*

Theron spread his arms and legs out. His wingsuit snapped open, and he slowed a little. *Sienna!* Where was she? Alarm rocketed through him. They had to bleed off as much speed as they could, or they'd hit the ground too fast.

He arched his head back and spotted her, her illusion system off as Roth had warned them. Instantly, everything in him settled. She was in perfect form, her wingsuit out, and focused on her descent. That was his girl.

The wingsuits had excellent maneuverability. Theron angled toward the closest trees lining the nearby hills, and away from the aliens.

The ground rushed up at them. He felt his high-tech wingsuit go rigid and expand even farther, slowing him more.

But it wasn't enough. They were still coming in fast. *Shit.* Theron braced himself. This was going to hurt.

He crashed into the ground, rolling over and over. Finally, he came to a stop not far from some trees. *God.* He lay there for a second, stunned. He pushed up on his hands and knees, shaking his head to clear it. He tentatively moved his arms and legs, and nothing appeared broken, or badly injured.

He sat up, searching for Sienna. She was several meters away, face down on the ground. Not moving.

"Sienna!" He pushed to his feet and ran to her.

Dropping to his knees, he rolled her over. Her hair had escaped its tie, and he pushed the mass of curls off her face. Blood covered the side of her face, and his heart stopped.

Then she groaned and coughed. "I'm okay."

He probed the cut on her cheekbone. Her eyes were still closed, but the sound of her voice made his rapidly drumming heart settle a little.

"Did we make it?" she asked.

He patted down her body, checking for any injuries. "Yeah. We made it. You have a nasty cut on your cheek."

She opened her eyes and he cupped her face, needing to touch her.

She groaned once more. "Let's not do that again, either."

"Deal. Now we need to hide. The aliens will come

looking for us." He lifted his head, scanning the trees.

Sienna sat up, grimacing. "We should hike into the mountains and head north until we can get back in comms range with the Enclave. Most of this area is national park. I'm pretty sure there are a few places where there were camping areas and accommodation."

He nodded, pulling her to her feet. "And we know the raptors don't like the trees, so we stay in them as much as possible."

Together, they pulled the remnants of their wingsuits off. It only took him a second to realize the illusion system on his armor was no longer working. Sienna watched him with a worried gaze.

"Must have been damaged in the fall." He shrugged. "No time to worry about it, we need to keep moving."

With arms around each other, they hiked to the top of the first hill. When they reached a small clearing, they looked back and had a perfect view down to the valley and of the hydro-electric power station.

As Theron took in the mass of aliens, he wished he had a camera. He tried to memorize the entire scene in front of him.

"They've tapped into the power station," Sienna said. "See the cables over there...they're running out to where those creepers are gathered."

This had to play a part in the Gizzida's plan. Something to do with the aliens' secret weapon to wipe out humanity.

She stared down in the valley. "What are they doing?"

Theron gripped the back of her neck. "Trying to wipe us out for good."

He felt her stiffen. "We keep fighting and surviving, but we're still no closer to being rid of the Gizzida."

He squeezed. "Hey, we don't give up."

She nodded.

"We stand up." He spun her to face him. "For our home, our friends, for those we've lost." He thought of his parents, his family, his fellow Rangers. "For our future."

Her gaze locked with his. "What's in our future, Theron?"

"Love."

She smiled. "Is that worth fighting for?"

He tightened his arms around her. "Hell, yeah."

Her smile widened. "You stealing Hell Squad's battle cry?"

"Maybe."

Then her smile faded and her gaze moved over his shoulder. "Raptor patrol heading this way."

Theron turned. A big, squat, black vehicle with spikes on it was bouncing along the valley floor in their direction.

He pulled her into the trees. "We'll head north. It'll take us a few days to hike back to the Enclave."

She nodded, circling a tree. "Our squad will be looking for us."

"Of course they will." Roth and Squad Nine wouldn't abandon them. "They'll send a drone south until they pick up the trackers in our armor." They just had to survive until then.

They jogged through the trees, moving back down a hill. At the bottom, the trees thinned out, and a narrow road snaked between the slopes.

Theron had just taken one step out onto the road, when he heard engines gunning.

He swiveled, snatching his carbine off his shoulder. A raptor vehicle was speeding down the road toward them. Behind it were several raptor patrols sprinting their way.

"How did they find us?" Sienna yelled, lifting her own weapon.

A thousand curses ran through Theron's head, but he reached deep for some control. "Run, Sienna. Into the trees."

"No."

"Go!" He injected every ounce of command that he could.

She stepped up beside him. "You just told me that what we have is worth fighting for."

"Damn you for being so courageous."

"I love you, too."

As the lead raptor vehicle pulled closer, they opened fire together.

Chapter Fifteen

The raptor vehicle gunned closer.

Sienna kept firing, but their carbines were barely making a dent in the armored vehicle. Three large spikes rose up from the front of it, making it look like some charging dinosaur.

It skidded to a stop nearby, raptor soldiers jumping out of it.

There were too many. "Let's go that way!" She nodded to the trees.

Theron sprayed another round of laser fire, then they started running. Just a few meters until they were in the relative safety of the trees.

Suddenly, she heard a *thwap* sound from behind them. A net fell over her and she slammed into the ground.

No. She struggled against the organic black fibers, and saw Theron lunge to the side to run her way. "No, keep going!"

Another net launched and it exploded around Theron. He tripped and rolled across the ground.

Despair crashed over her. Theron roared, struggling to get out of his net. She reached down and pulled out her combat knife. She sliced at the fibers, but they were too damn strong.

Two booted feet stepped right in front of her face. She looked up into the ugly, gray-scaled face of a raptor. He bared his teeth at her, his demonic eyes glowing. Several other raptors appeared.

Sienna was yanked up and dragged toward the raptor vehicle. She had a perfect view of two raptors hauling Theron up. He kicked out, the net hampering him, but managed to knock one alien over.

The second one landed an unforgiving punch to Theron's mid-section. She bit her lip and watched as he grunted and doubled over. She knew his armor would protect him a bit, but it still had to hurt.

She was tossed into the back of the raptor vehicle. A second later, Theron landed beside her.

She struggled upward. "Are you okay?"

"Fine."

The back door slammed shut and they were plunged into darkness. She felt the vehicle rock from side to side, and figured the raptors were climbing in the front.

She reached out a hand, her fingers brushing his. The vehicle pulled away.

"You should have run," Theron ground out.

"I'd never leave you."

He yanked her close and she wished she could see him. She cupped his cheeks through the net, loving the scrape of his stubble.

"I lost everyone." His voice was ragged. "I failed everyone I cared about. I can't lose you, too."

Her heart hurt for him. "Theron, you didn't fail

anyone. Your parents, your siblings, your fellow Rangers...the aliens killed them." She slid her hands into his hair. "I told you once before that you have a hero buried under your quiet toughness. You try to protect everyone around you, but that doesn't mean it is your responsibility to save everyone."

His hands cupped her head, his breathing harsh. "I've never been good enough. I was born with darkness in me."

Sienna mentally cursed the woman who'd scarred him as a young child. "*Cazzate*. Bullshit. We are all dark and light, good and bad. That's what makes us human. You don't need to be perfect to be loved, Theron. You don't have to be a shining good guy to be worthy of love. I love you as you are. All the black, white, and gray in you."

He made a sound and yanked her close, his mouth capturing hers. She drank him in, her hands digging into his shoulders. She didn't know what they'd face when this vehicle stopped, but whatever it was, they'd face it together.

They held each other in the darkness during the long, bumpy ride. Finally, the vehicle pulled to a halt.

The back doors opened, the sunlight blinding them. The next thing she knew, she was yanked out and dropped onto the ground. Theron, still covered in his net, was dumped beside her.

Sienna's eyesight adjusted. They were right in front of the hydro-electric power station, and surrounded by raptor troops.

She listened to the raptors discussing them and gesturing. One raptor was slightly taller than the others and appeared to be in charge. Sienna kept her face blank, ready to face whatever happened next. She glanced at Theron. His face looked like granite, and she saw him subtly scanning their surroundings, assessing, planning, thinking.

Two raptors yanked Sienna up to her feet. One drew a huge black blade with a jagged edge. She sucked in a breath and stiffened her spine.

"Leave her alone." Theron started struggling, and four raptors circled him, holding him in place.

The raptor in front of her cut the net off her, then slid the knife away. She blew out a breath, watching as Theron's net was cut away, too. Then clawed hands tore at them, yanking their armor off, and taking their weapons. Finally, they stood there in only their cargo pants and T-shirts. Even in the late afternoon sun, she felt chilled. Their odds of survival were looking pretty grim.

She drew herself up and looked at the tall raptor. "What are—?"

He took a step forward and backhanded her.

Sienna flew backward and hit the ground. Her face throbbed. *Ow.*

Theron surged forward, but another raptor whacked the butt of his weapon against Theron's gut, knocking him back a step. Cursing, Theron grabbed Sienna and pulled her close.

His hand smoothed over her cheek. "Okay?"

She nodded. The big alien had turned his back on them, seemingly ignoring them. Then he barked out an order and several raptors took off at a jog.

The big raptor looked at them now. She saw him take in the way Theron was holding her, and the alien's head tilted. If she had to guess, he looked confused.

The Gizzida cared about strength and domination. They had no clue about caring or love.

Warmth burst inside her. And that would be their downfall. Fear and power could only take you so far. They had no understanding of the motivation of love. Of deep love that completed and nurtured, like what she felt for Theron. Of the ferocious love of a mother, who would do anything to see her children safe. Of the love of family and friends, who would stick together and always fight for each other.

"Any chance you see to get out, you take it," Theron murmured.

Right. She could race through an army of raptors, unarmed, with no armor. *Piece of cake.*

There was a small commotion, and the crowd of raptors parted.

She felt Theron tense beside her, and Sienna hissed out a breath. Several raptors were leading in a herd of creepers. The skittish creatures were screeching and fighting their chains.

Suddenly, the lead creeper stopped, and let out an ear-splitting screech. Sienna slapped her hands over her ears and saw several raptors back up a few steps. The alien's belly was glowing brightly, and was far more distended then the other creeper she'd seen on the alien ship.

The creature started shaking, and a second later, its belly detached and dropped to the ground.

Horrified, Sienna just stared. Dimly, she heard Theron curse.

The creeper had just *laid* a pod. What the hell was going on here?

"Help! Help me!"

A man's screams made Sienna turn. A human was dragged forward by two raptors. He was dropped on the ground.

"Help." His hair was disheveled and his clothes torn.

Sienna's eyes widened. "Howell?"

The former United Coalition President just stared at her, his eyes wild. He didn't appear to recognize anything, too lost in his terror. She'd thought he was dead.

Then a creeper skittered forward, and leaned down toward the man. Theron snatched Sienna back, and she watched as the creeper's mouth opened wide. It sucked the terrified man up in one gulp.

Oh, hell no. Sienna blinked. The creeper had just *eaten* Howell whole. This was like some terrible horror movie. She saw the creeper's stomach expand, and inside, she could see the silhouette of a man struggling.

Realization was a horrible spill of ice down her spine. She looked at the creepers, then at the sea of orange pods surrounding them.

"They don't need the genesis tanks anymore," she whispered. She knew the transformation from human to Gizzida in the tanks took months. "They've engineered another way to turn us into them."

A muscle ticked in Theron's jaw as he stared at the creeper that had swallowed Howell. "Fuck, no."

Raptors moved forward and knocked Theron to his knees. Sienna got a sharp blow in her lower back and fell down beside him.

Then she looked up and saw two creepers with flat, empty bellies being led toward them.

Her gut cramped and she grasped Theron's hand. "Theron."

***

Theron felt like his body was encased in ice. When they'd driven here in the raptor vehicle, he'd imagined being tortured, fighting, pain. Not *this*.

No way he was letting Sienna be eaten by an alien and then turned into one.

"Sienna, I'll cause a diversion."

She looked up at him and snorted. "While I run and leave you to be swallowed whole by an alien?"

He saw the fear and horror in her eyes, but clearly that wasn't enough to get her to listen to his plan. She wouldn't leave. "And you call me stubborn."

"I've been learning from the best. I have a better idea." She nodded her head to the left.

Theron looked that way and saw several of the giant exosuits that the aliens had been using to shift cargo. These weren't in use, and were standing open, waiting for an operator.

Risky. Even if they could reach them, there was no guarantee that he and Sienna could operate the alien technology.

But, they might offer some protection, and if they could get them working...at least they could go down fighting, and not stuck in the belly of an alien.

He squeezed her hand. "Sienna, I love you."

Her eyebrows shot up. "You decide to tell me *now?* Surrounded by raptors, and about to be eaten by creepers?"

"Sorry. Seems I have a problem with good timing when it comes to you."

"Luckily, I love you, too." Her lips tilted up. "Now, are you ready to fight?"

One of the creepers moved closer to them and let out a screech.

"Oh, yeah." Theron lunged to his feet, knocking into the raptor guard beside him. He grabbed the alien's weapon, spun it around, and opened fire. He sprayed green poison over the creepers and other raptors.

Chaos.

Raptors shouted and dived. The creepers screeched and tried to run, trampling over other raptors, yanking the keepers who didn't immediately let go of their leashes along with them.

Theron turned, and saw Sienna sprinting toward the exosuits. He laid down another round of fire.

But he could see the raptors were regrouping.

Come on, Sienna. He glanced over his shoulder, and saw her leap into the closest exosuit. He watched the bone-like suit close around her.

Theron kept firing, steadily walking backward toward the other exosuits. Suddenly, the raptor weapon jammed, no more poison spraying out of it.

Fuck. He tossed the gun at the incoming raptors and sprinted toward the suits. He dived into the one beside Sienna's. The suit closed around him, and red lights flared to life on the controls right in front of his face.

It was covered in raptor-scrawl, and he couldn't make heads or tails out of the controls. There were buttons, some levers, and a pad that felt sticky.

Something hit his suit, and he heard sizzling. The raptors had almost reached him, and were firing.

Come on. He pressed buttons and symbols on the screen, trying to get the suit to do *something*.

The raptor patrol was almost on top of him.

Suddenly, a huge figure stomped in front of his suit. He watched the giant arms of the other exosuit swing and slam into the incoming raptors. Several bodies flew through the air.

Sienna. She'd worked out her controls and, as he watched, she waded into the raptors, stomping the exosuit's giant legs down on aliens and swinging the arms. He grinned. She was his sprinkle-coated badass, all right.

Theron turned his attention back to the controls. He touched more buttons, and finally, his suit moved. A few more tests, and he worked out some of the basic controls. He touched a lever, and his exosuit moved forward with lumbering steps.

He stomped up beside Sienna, and joined the fight.

Together, they swung, hit, and smashed anything they could touch. They tore through raptor after raptor, and smashed through several orange pods, goo splattering everywhere.

Theron took a moment to look beyond the immediate skirmish. They were carving a pretty good path toward the edge of the alien encampment.

Adrenaline flooded him. Now, they had a chance. Maybe they could actually break through and escape.

"Head that way!" He used his exosuit arm to point. Through the amber panel that formed the suit's eye slit, he could see her nodding.

They kept fighting raptors. Theron took great pleasure in stomping over a few creepers.

Then he saw something that chilled his soul.

A row of raptor vehicles was lining up in front of them, forming a barrier.

He glanced at Sienna and saw her face was grim.

"I love you," he shouted at her.

She pressed a hand to the glass on her suit and her lips moved. "I love you, too."

Ahead, he watched, as all the cannons mounted on the raptor vehicles swung in their direction.

He wouldn't lose Sienna. He wouldn't let her die

here. "I'll fight for you," he vowed. "Until I can't fight anymore."

Chapter Sixteen

Sienna grimly touched the controls, starting her exosuit toward the vehicles.

The suits didn't have any weapons.

The nearest vehicle's cannon opened fire. Flames exploded around her, and she tensed. Then she relaxed. She hadn't been hit.

Then she looked over at Theron's exosuit and her heart sank.

Through the smoke, she saw his suit was staggering backward. The bone-like chest plate was torn up and damaged.

"No," she whispered. Then, the smoke cleared, and she saw he was okay, but his suit was failing.

It couldn't sustain another hit.

Helplessness rushed over her. They were out of options. Her hands tightened on the controls. It looked like she wasn't going to get her happily-ever-after, after all. God, why couldn't she and Theron have realized what they meant to each other earlier?

She took a step forward in her exosuit and watched another cannon preparing to fire.

She straightened her spine and pressed her shoulders back. Whatever happened, she would go down fighting for herself and the man she loved.

Suddenly, there was another explosion, flames blossoming skyward, rocks, gravel, and debris spraying in all directions. As Sienna watched, a raptor vehicle was tossed into the air, flames pluming from it.

Her chest tightened and she looked up, catching three small, fast shimmers passing overhead.

Darkswifts.

Excitement and relief zinged through her. Their squad had arrived.

Green laser fire traced through the air, hitting the raptor vehicles, sending another one up in flames.

A second later, several Hawks appeared in the sky, dropping their illusions as they neared the ground. One hovered only a few meters away from her.

Sienna plowed through some raptors, positioning herself to protect the quadcopter, and saw Hell Squad and Squad Three leaping out of the Hawks.

She saw Marcus throw out an arm and shout. She didn't need to hear his gravelly voice to know what he was saying.

Ready to go to hell?

Around him, his squad shouted and leaped into the fight. *Hell, yeah! The devil needs an ass-kicking.*

With adrenaline surging, Sienna moved forward, kicking and punching with her exosuit. Beside her, Theron was doing the same.

Together, they trampled through raptors and creepers. Across the space, their gazes met, and they grinned at each other.

All of a sudden, a missile flew from a raptor vehicle, and slammed directly into the chest of Theron's suit. His suit was flung backward in a ball of flames and smoke.

Sienna's heart stopped. She knew the suit couldn't withstand another hit. "Theron!"

***

Hemi

Hemi Rahia fired his carbine, his focus on taking down the aliens.

Fucking Gizzida. The bastards had invaded the world, and killed and destroyed millions. He had zero issues mowing them down.

He yanked a grenade off his belt and lobbed it into a group of approaching raptors. He grinned. As flames erupted, his squad fanned out around him, firing at the aliens.

They were the toughest sons of bitches he'd ever fought with, and he was proud to stand with them.

"Think I'm going to have this year's quota for the most kills," Levi called out. The former biker, aimed his carbine, taking down two raptors in quick succession.

Hemi snorted and yanked his shotgun off his back. "You wish, King." A raptor charged at Hemi with a roar, and Hemi pumped the weapon, then shot the alien in the gut.

"Incoming!" Tane yelled.

A raptor grenade bounced between them—an ugly, black device covered in spikes. Hemi and his squad mates dived out of the way.

He hit the ground and rolled, just as flames exploded behind him. He came to his feet and realized he'd been separated from the other guys.

Several raptors were moving in to surround him.

He pumped the shotgun. "Bring it on, assholes." He shot the nearest raptor, the boom echoing around him.

A huge-ass creeper skittered closer and let out a screech. Damn thing was so ugly. He pumped the shotgun again.

Suddenly, laser fire sprayed the beast, cutting it down.

Hemi looked up and saw the Darkswift shoot past.

"Looked like you needed some help." The smug female voice came through his earpiece.

"Baby, I was doing just fine, but I know you can't stay away from me."

He easily pictured Cam's long, lean body settled in the Darkswift, and he easily pictured her nose scrunching from his comment. He waited for her snarky response.

A half snort, half laugh crossed the comm line and he realized Cam's partner, Taylor, was on the line as well.

"Keep dreaming, Rahia." Cam's tone was sharp.

Ah, there it was. It was really sick, he knew, but

he loved when she tossed that attitude his way.

He paused to shoot another raptor, and headed back toward his squad. "I've got plenty of dreams, Cam." He lowered his voice. "And you star in all of them." And it was about damn time she quit running and he made them more than just dreams.

A humming silence.

He grinned. Yeah, he loved poking at her and seeing her flares of passion and temper.

"Rahia, if you think—"

He cut her off. "It's New Year's Eve soon." He kicked a dying raptor out of his way. "There's a big party planned and at the stroke of twelve, I'll find you."

"Oh?" A slow, unconcerned drawl.

"The kiss at midnight is all mine." You're all mine. It was a promise.

"Keep dreaming, Rahia," she snapped.

As more raptors converged, he swung his weapon around. Oh, he would. And he had every intention of making his dreams come true.

***

Theron tried to move. His ears were ringing, and his vision was blurry.

He was flat on his back, some of the damaged shell of the exosuit still around him. He looked down and saw the shattered pieces of the suit rammed into his chest.

Dimly, he wondered why that didn't hurt.

He tried to move again, but he didn't have the

strength, and he was trapped by the remains of the suit.

"Theron!" Sienna's pretty face appeared above him. She gripped the ruined suit, pulling parts of it off him.

She was out of her suit. She was putting herself at risk. "Get back in your exosuit!"

"No." Her horrified gaze was on his torn chest and stomach. She touched it gingerly. "Oh, Theron."

Theron could feel the blood soaking into his clothes now. A wave of tiredness washed over him. "You are the best thing that's ever happened to me, Sienna. Please stay safe."

Her lips trembled, and he saw tears in her eyes.

"You aren't damn well saying goodbye. I'm getting you out of here, and rescuing you, Big T."

The pain was starting now. He drew in a deep breath. This was going to suck. "Sienna—"

"Just be quiet." She pulled more of the bone plating off. "I'm the boss right now." Then she sucked in a sharp breath.

Theron looked down. A large shaft of bone was sticking out of his gut.

"Theron." Her face went white. She reached up and touched his cheek.

"It's too late for me, naughty girl. Get to safety."

She shook her head, tears brimming.

"Get to Hell Squad." He heard carbine fire nearby, and the shouts of his fellow soldiers.

She swiped a hand at her eyes. "You think I'm too soft and sweet to save the life of the stubborn man I love?"

"No. I know my woman is *courageous* and will fight to the end." He fought back a moan at the wave of pain. "You terrify me."

Suddenly, a dark shape reared up behind her. "Sienna! Raptor!"

She threw herself to the side and rolled away. He saw her face the raptor, ducking the alien's swings. Without her armor, she was no match for the bastard.

Theron tried to move, but agony tore through him. He fell back, panting and helpless. There was no way he could help her.

Sienna slid into a crouch, and grabbed one of the shards of bone from his ruined exosuit. She brandished it like a sword, and when the raptor attacked again, she swung it like a bat, slamming the jagged edge into the raptor's face.

He roared and fell to his knees. Face grim, Sienna attacked him, again and again. Her blows were relentless. The raptor toppled over like a felled tree.

She lowered the bone shard, her chest heaving. Theron had never seen anything in his entire life as sexy as his Sienna.

"Looks like you don't need a rescue."

Sienna lifted the bone, ready to attack again.

Theron recognized Shaw's amused drawl. As Hell Squad's sniper stepped into view, Theron felt the tension in him slide away. Sienna was safe.

Claudia appeared, her carbine held in one hand and a med kit in the other. She set the kit down beside Theron. "You look like you need a rescue, though, big guy."

Theron managed a nod. "It's been a hell of a day."

Sienna knelt beside him, grabbing his hand. "We survived collapsing buildings, jumped from an alien ship, almost got swallowed by an alien creature, and Theron told me he loves me."

Claudia grinned and pressed an injector against his neck. Instantly, he felt the meds kicking in.

"Well, that is eventful. You're going to need a big shot of nanomeds." Claudia held up a vial of the small medical machines. "I won't lie, this is going to hurt a lot."

He smiled goofily at Sienna. "Hold my hand?"

She was fighting back a weak laugh. "Wow, out of everything in the world, you're bad with meds?"

The rest of Hell Squad appeared, and Marcus stepped forward, his armor splattered with blood and gore. "Aliens are retreating, but they'll be back. We took them by surprise, but once they regroup, we'll lose the advantage." He glanced at Theron, his face serious. "Can we move him?"

Claudia nodded. "Give me a minute to get these nanomeds in."

From nearby, Shaw whistled. "Did you guys hear? Theron's taken the fall."

When Claudia shot Shaw a narrowed look, her lover cleared his throat.

"It's a great ride, man. Enjoy." Shaw winked. "You sure picked a pretty one."

"She is pretty, isn't she?" Theron heard the slur

in his voice. Pain spiked everywhere, as the nanomeds rushed into his veins, but with Sienna beside him, he didn't care. "She's all mine. And she looks even prettier with my pink palm marks all over her curvy ass."

Sienna gasped. She pressed her palm over Theron's mouth as the others laughed.

Even Marcus was fighting a smile. "Let's get you guys home."

***

Sienna balanced the tray with one hand, and managed to get the door to her room open with the other. She stepped inside, and found Theron sitting on the edge of the bed.

"Hey." She set the tray down on the table and rushed forward. "You are supposed to be taking it easy." She nudged him back against the pillows.

He scowled at her, his favorite expression nowadays, as she reached behind him to fluff the pillows.

"Sienna, I'm fine. I'm all healed."

"Doc Emerson said you needed to rest. You were badly injured." Her own chest hitched, remembering the Hawk ride back to the Enclave, watching as Theron had slipped into unconsciousness. The nanomeds had healed him, but she still woke sometimes in a cold sweat.

"You've had me chained to the bed for two days." His scowl deepened. "And not in the fun way."

Sienna had also banned sex until he was better.

It appeared that ban was making her Big T a little grumpier than usual.

She turned back to the table. "I brought you some dinner. Pizza with salami and basil." She moved the tray to the bedside table. She wiggled her eyebrows. "Extra spicy. And a glass of red wine. My nonna used to always say, a meal without wine is a day without sunshine."

Theron cupped her cheek. "I couldn't live without the sunshine."

God, the man knew how to make her melt.

"Any update from Roth?" he asked.

Sienna fussed with the tray. "No. The drone and intel team are working overtime to try and find out more about the creepers. Hell Squad brought back some samples." She grimaced. "They are apparently some sort of alien creature augmented with human DNA, as well as DNA from several Earth animals."

"Shit."

She nodded. "The general thinks that the raptors have been experimenting all this time. Using the local wildlife to find a way to fine-tune their process of turning everyone into raptors. Gaz'da has confirmed that on each planet they invade, they adapt their processes to the indigenous species."

"So now they'll unleash creepers on us?"

Not a pleasant thought. "It doesn't matter what they unleash." She grabbed his hand. "We keep fighting. For those we've lost, for friends and family, for ourselves."

"Always," he promised.

"They told Howell's wife what happened to him." Sienna almost felt sorry for the man.

Theron shrugged a shoulder. "He brought it on himself."

She nodded. "I can't stop thinking about his poor wife and kids."

A hand cupped her jaw. "My sweet, kind-hearted Sienna."

She smiled, banishing the unpleasant thoughts. "Oh, I forgot to tell you what else I brought you." She whipped a napkin off the top of the second bowl. "One bowl of chocolate ice cream. No syrup, no nuts, no sprinkles."

He reached out and grabbed her wrist. "I want sprinkles. I want sprinkles every day for the rest of my life."

Sienna's breath hitched. He made her so happy, and when he looked at her, she knew he saw all of her, and loved every part of her equally. "That can be arranged."

She hurried over to her small kitchenette, and grabbed the sprinkles he'd given her. She set them down beside his ice cream. "So, I—"

Theron yanked her onto the bed and she let out a loud squeak.

He pulled her facedown across his lap. "Theron, the doc said—"

"Screw the doc. I'm fine." He landed a stinging slap to Sienna's butt.

She moaned, instant desire flooding her. God, he could have her ready in just seconds. He tore her shorts off and paused. He slid a finger under the black lace, fingering the elastic. "You wear this for me?"

"You gave it to me."

He spanked her again, and she writhed. "So I did. I knew your sexy little ass would look perfect in them." Another sharp slap, followed by the caress of his palm.

His hand slid between her thighs, and as he sank his fingers inside her, she let out a mewling cry and surrendered herself up to the pleasure. "Love me, Theron."

"I do. Completely. With everything I am."

Then, he flipped her over, and the next thing she felt was something cool against her belly. She gasped and looked down to see a dollop of chocolate ice cream on her skin. "Theron!"

Next, he upended the sprinkles, coating her with the colored bits of sugar. "There, now that's perfect."

She giggled, but as he leaned down, his mouth licking at the ice cream on her skin, her giggles turned to moans. He pulled her up on top of him, forcing her to straddle his hips.

He sank back, lounging like a king on the pillows. He had a hard, commanding look that would suit a monarch used to getting his own way. "Now take my cock out, climb on, and sink down on it. I want to watch it stretching you wide."

The air caught in her lungs, and her hands went to pull his trousers down.

Sienna rose above him and sank down on him,

taking every hard inch of him inside her. A groan ripped from his throat, and his hands clamped on her hips.

"God, I love you, Sienna," he ground out between gritted teeth. He forced her to move faster, harder. They lost themselves in loving each other.

A while later, Sienna climbed out of the bed on wobbly legs. A few places ached and stung in the sweetest way. Theron was still lounging, with just the sheet pulled to his waist, looking well-satisfied and pleased with himself.

She let her gaze drift over his bare chest. There was no sign of the horrible injuries he'd suffered, although he still had a few odd scars, here and there. Her man was a soldier through and through.

No, he didn't look like a king, she decided. He would be the captain of the king's guard. Always ready to fight and protect.

She hurried into the bathroom and washed up, pulling on her blue robe. Now, she had to bully her man into eating, and not let him get her naked again.

When she reentered the bedroom, his hot hazel gaze was on her. "Come here."

The command in his voice made her shiver. "You need to eat now."

"I will. You."

God. Heat flooded her. She took one step toward the bed—

There was a sharp knock, followed by the door immediately opening. Cam sauntered in, followed by the rest of their squad. Avery, Niko, and Devlin were also part of the crowd.

"We decided it was time to come and check on you," Cam announced. She eyed Theron on the bed and then Sienna in her robe. "Apparently, you're doing just fine."

"My eyes," Roth grumbled as he sat at the table. He set down a six-pack of homebrews.

"Mmm, I smell pizza." Taylor grabbed the box from the bedside table, and flicked it open.

"Share," Mac ordered.

Teasing laughter filled the room. With a shake of her head, Sienna headed for the bed. "Cam, call the kitchen. I left a few uncooked pizzas in the fridge. Tell them to pop them in the oven."

"On it."

Sienna was sure her mama would approve of the family she'd made for herself. Theron pulled her down beside him, and she snuggled into his strength. And of the man she'd fallen in love with. Somehow, she'd ended up with everything she'd ever dreamed about.

"*Amare e non essere amato, quanto risponde sens esser chiamato,*" she murmured.

Theron pressed his cheek against her hair. "You know it always turns me on when you speak Italian. What's it mean?"

It was the perfect saying for how she felt. "To love and be loved as it is meant to be."

I hope you enjoyed Theron and Sienna's story!

Hell Squad continues with HEMI, starring the first of the big, wild berserkers of Squad Three.

Read on for a preview of the first chapter.

Don't miss out! For updates about new releases, action romance info, free books, and other fun stuff, sign up for my VIP mailing list and get your *free box set* containing three action-packed romances.

Visit here to get started:
www.annahackettbooks.com

FREE BOX SET DOWNLOAD

JOIN THE ACTION-PACKED ADVENTURE!

Formats: Kindle, ePub, PDF

Preview – Hell Squad: Hemi

"I cannot *believe* that moron," Camryn McNab muttered.

From behind her on the Hawk quadcopter, she heard snickers from her squad mates. She whipped around to glare at them. God, even their leader—rough, rugged Roth Masters—was grinning.

"It is not funny," she insisted.

"I think it looks pretty," Sienna said. The small, curvy brunette looked like she should be in a kitchen baking, not decked out in carbon fiber armor, about to head into a battle with invading dinosaur-like aliens.

Cam pointed to the combat helmet on her head. "He put an *H* on my helmet...in *rhinestones*." Even though she couldn't see the offending letter, anger was a wild churn in her belly. The man could light the fuse on her temper faster than anyone she'd ever known. "And he glued them on with some high-tech adhesive." When they'd been prepping for their mission, and she'd discovered the tampering, she'd tried to pry the rhinestones off, but they weren't budging.

At the back of the Hawk, Taylor Cates started laughing. Her dark hair was pulled back in a ponytail and as she doubled over, it fell over her shoulder. "Can you picture big, bad Hemi with sparkly rhinestones?" She held her middle as she laughed.

Beside Taylor, their second-in-command, Mackenna 'Mac' Carides, was biting her lip to fight back a laugh. Hell, even quiet, stubborn Theron was smiling. He'd been doing that a lot these last few days, since he and Sienna had turned from friends to lovers.

"Go ahead, laugh it up," Cam said darkly.

Hemi Rahia, bane of her existence, wouldn't know what hit him when she got back to base.

He was a soldier on Squad Three—a group of men also known as the berserkers, for their wild fighting style. He was also a big, muscled, tattooed, aggravating moron.

"Coming up on the targets," a male voice called back from the cockpit. Their top Hawk pilot, Finn Erickson, was at the controls today. Beneath her, Cam felt the quadcopter move into a turn.

Cam put any thought of pranks, revenge, and Hemi out of her head. It was time to focus on their mission.

Over a year and a half ago, aliens had invaded Earth. Almost overnight, she'd gone from a member of the United Coalition Airforce's Combat Support Squadron, protecting airfields, aircraft and personnel, to a member of Squad Nine.

Home was now a former underground coal mine, called the Enclave. All the fighting squads were made up of survivors from former military and police groups, or—in the case of the berserkers— people from questionable backgrounds who knew how to fight. Her squad consisted of a bunch of kickass ladies, their fearless leader Roth, and big, quiet Theron. They were tight, and she was proud as hell that they made an awesome team.

Now, they fought to protect the inhabitants of the Enclave, as well as to defeat the Gizzida. Her jaw tightened, and she pressed a hand against the wall of the Hawk. Cam liked fighting back. She looked out the side window at the setting sun. It was New Year's Eve, and she had no idea what the new year would bring. None of them did.

Would they finally be able to beat the Gizzida, and all the strange and terrifying creatures they used as weapons? Would humanity survive to rebuild their world?

She shook her head. Her thoughts were turning far too melancholy and deep.

"Let's get this mission done." They were off to destroy a large pack of hellions—alien hunting dogs, with poison-filled bellies. She straightened and looked at her friends. "I want to get back for the big party tonight."

Everyone at the Enclave was excited for the party. She knew how important it was for everyone to blow off a little steam, and celebrate all the little good things that they still managed to find in the middle of this alien apocalypse. Cam wanted to drink, dance, and find some hottie to kiss at midnight.

She recalled a certain moron had taunted her on

their last mission to rescue Theron and Sienna from an alien encampment. In alpha-male style, he'd already claimed her New Year's kiss.

In your dreams, Rahia.

"I want to get back to the party, too," a deep voice said, interrupting her thoughts.

Cam narrowed her eyes suspiciously on Theron. The man hated parties. "You just want to bang Sienna's brains out."

Theron tilted his head, his face thoughtful. "Yep."

Since her friends had hooked up, they'd been inseparable. They were so damn perfect together. The big man and the sweet soldier. Cam saw pink fill Sienna's cheeks as she stared at her man.

It was sweet, but it wasn't for Cam. *No, no, no.* She was *not* built for long-term. Fun, easy, and sexy...that was what she liked, and frankly, all she could manage. She came from two people incapable of love.

No. That wasn't true. Her parents were only capable of toxic, soul-destroying love.

She felt the Hawk start to descend. Out the window, she could see a strange, red-orange glow ahead.

Roth shouldered in beside her. "What the hell is that?"

They were south of the Enclave, but the landscape still consisted of rolling, green hills. Between two hills was a large, pockmarked patch of ground. It looked like it had been bombarded by meteors. Each of the holes glowed orange from underground.

It reminded Cam of a trip she'd taken to Hawaii once, to see the lava field near the volcano on the Big Island.

But she knew this strangeness had nothing to do with volcanoes and everything to do with the aliens.

"Whatever it is, it's not our priority," Roth said. "I'll pass the intel on. For now, the drone team reported a large group of hellions in the area, and they're getting too close to the Enclave. We need to clean them out."

Mac swung her carbine off her shoulder. "Let's do this."

Moments later, the Hawk was hovering above the ground and Roth slid the side door open with one powerful shove. "Time to go hunting."

Cam leaped out, her boots hitting the grass. The sunset had turned the western horizon brilliant shades of orange and pink. She raised her carbine, the feel of it familiar under her gloved hands. She moved into formation with her squad, falling in behind Mac.

"Anyone see the hellions?" Mac murmured.

Cam saw green grass, clumps of trees in the distance near a farmhouse, and that eerie orange glow in the distance, but no mangy beasts.

"Squad Nine." The cool, feminine voice came through their earpieces. Arden was their comms officer, who sat back at base, feeding them intel. "You have a pack of ten hellions inbound."

"Ten?" Sienna shuddered.

"Be ready," Roth said, tone hard.

"There!" Mac yelled.

Off to the left, Cam heard the yips and snarls. A pack of scaled, spiked, alien dogs was bounding toward them. Each animal had a powerful body, spikes along its back, slavering jaws filled with sharp teeth, and glowing-red bellies filled with poison.

Squad Nine opened fire, green laser blasts whizzing through the twilight. Cam aimed, taking down the first alien hunting dog. Its belly burst open, spraying out corrosive red fluid. Other hellions fell, their angry snarls and howls of pain filling the air.

"Grenades out." Theron's deep voice.

Cam watched as the grenades sailed through the air. They were made with cedar oil, which for whatever reason, the hellions and the closely-related canids, found strongly repulsive.

As the grenades exploded, sending up a fine mist, she watched the hellions scatter in a chaotic frenzy, spinning and snapping at each other. Several turned and ran into the growing darkness.

"Take them down," Roth ordered.

"On it." Taylor was down on one knee, holding a long-range laser rifle. Cam watched as, one by one, the fleeing dogs fell. Taylor was good. She might even give Hell Squad's charming sniper, Shaw Baird, a run for his money.

"More hellions coming in from behind you," Arden said.

As soon as Arden spoke, a low growl reached

Cam's ears. She spun and spotted the incoming hellions.

"On our six," Cam called out.

She fired on the animals, but these particular ones had wised up. They dodged the laser fire, bounding closer.

Roth lunged past her, a large combat knife in his hand. As one giant hellion leaped at him, he jumped into the air to meet it.

Roth was a badass. Cam swung her carbine onto her shoulder, and pulled her dual laser pistols from the holsters on her thighs.

As the other hellion came at her, she held her weapons up, walking calmly toward the creature as she fired.

Its belly exploded and she leaped back to avoid the sizzling poison. The red fluid splattered the ground, rapidly eating through the grass and dirt.

Cam turned and watched the final hellion fall under Sienna's carbine fire. Cam looked at Roth and saw him stand, then lean down to wipe the blood off his combat knife.

Cam sucked in a deep breath, adrenaline pumping thickly through her veins. Taylor smiled at her and Cam smiled back. All in a day's work for Squad Nine.

"All hellions on scans have been neutralized," Arden said. "Get back to base, Squad Nine."

"Arden, there is an area southwest of us," Roth said. "Pockmarked ground that's glowing orange. It has 'Gizzida' written all over it."

"Passing that intel on to the drone team. We'll

have them investigate." The cool, elegant woman rarely sounded flustered. "For now, it's getting dark, and there have been reports of alien swarms just south of your location. Time to get back to base."

Cam kicked the carcass of a hellion out of her way. She did not want to run into a swarm of bat-like aliens that could pick flesh off bones in seconds. At least the suckers only came out at night. "Plus, we have a party to get to."

"There's the Hawk." Roth waved them toward the incoming quadcopter.

The Hawk had dropped its illusion, its gray hull visible. As it descended, it kicked up dust around them.

Cam leaped aboard, followed by her squad mates. As the Hawk rose, she turned back to stare at the strange orange glow in the distance. For a second, she thought she saw shadows moving over the glow. Then Roth slammed the door closed.

Shaking off a sense of foreboding, she turned to her friends. "Party time, people."

Sienna dropped into a seat, grinning. "I've got a super-sexy dress to wear tonight."

Cam watched Theron's gaze sharpen on his woman. Smiling, Cam dropped into her own seat, stretching her long legs out in front of her. She had a sexy little dress of her own to wear tonight. Not that she was dressing up for anybody. Just herself.

However, if an annoying, helmet-interfering jerk happened to see her, she was going to make sure he got a good, long look at what he couldn't touch.

She closed her eyes. A party was just what she needed. She'd dance, get a little buzz from some homebrewed beer, and she'd find some fun in the middle of this shitty alien apocalypse.

***

Hemi Rahia strode up to the large double doors. They swooshed open and he stepped into the Enclave's Command Center.

His squad mates and his brothers were already down at the New Year's Eve party, but Hemi had something he needed to do first before he joined them.

Through a glass wall, he saw the drone team operators hunched over the controls of the drones out in the field. But he pulled his gaze back. He wasn't interested in the drones today. He spied some of the comms officers sitting in front of their comp screens, and zeroed in on one dark head.

"Hey, Arden."

At the deep rumble of his voice, the brunette swiveled, her eyes widening. "Hemi."

She was pretty, in a neat, elegant way. Not Hemi's style, he preferred attitude and fire. But the one thing that caught him was what he saw in her eyes—a heartbreaking sadness.

He cleared his throat. "I'm after an update on Squad Nine's mission."

"It went fine. They're on their way home, and eager to get to the party."

Something tight in Hemi's gut eased a little. "Good."

A small smile tilted Arden's lips. "I heard about the rhinestones."

Hemi shoved his hands in the pockets of his cargo pants. "How mad was she?"

Arden pressed her tongue to her teeth. "Mad."

Hemi grinned. *Good.* He and Camryn had been circling each other for months. Most days, it felt like a fucking lifetime. The woman had personal armor stronger than carbon fiber. And she could run. Hell, she had the legs for it, that was for sure.

But tonight, it stopped. Tonight was the beginning of a new year. It was time for him and Cam to begin new things.

"Thanks, Arden," he said. "See you at the party."

Her smile dissolved. "Maybe. Happy New Year, Hemi."

He headed out of the Command Center and down the corridor in the direction of the dining room, where the party was being held.

Hemi knew winning the war against the aliens was a long shot, but he also knew that he, his brothers, the other soldiers—they'd never stop fighting. They'd fight to keep kids safe, to protect the survivors who'd made it this far, to give humanity a chance.

But that didn't mean life didn't go on.

He thought of his mother. His Ma had lost her husband and been left to raise three rambunctious boys alone. She hadn't complained, she'd just gotten on with it. Surrounded by family back home in New Zealand, she'd made a home for him and his brothers. And eventually, she'd met a good man, and Hemi had scored an amazing stepdad who'd instilled in him a strong sense of right and wrong.

And his Pa had also given him a great example of how you treated the woman who was your everything.

Hemi liked women, and liked being buried deep inside their warmth and softness. God, they smelled sweet. But his Pa had told him that with the right one, the one who was worth the trouble, everything was so much better.

And Hemi knew Camryn McNab was his.

Every gorgeous, courageous, attitude-filled inch of her.

Now he had to convince her of that…if only he could get her to stop running.

He heard the music and laughter coming from the dining room. He pulled up short. The room had been transformed. Blue-and-silver fairy lights flickered all around the darkened room. A disco strobe light cast bright sparkles across the packed dance floor. A few older couples were swaying beside a group of teens bumping and grinding to the music.

All of the dining hall's tables and chairs had been moved to one side of the room, and a large number of people were sitting, eating and drinking. Nearby several long tables were filled with food. He saw a huge black man with one arm missing near the tables, barking orders at some of the kitchen staff. Chef had run the kitchens at their old base in the Blue Mountains. He'd been injured on their race to the Enclave, but he was clearly getting back on his feet.

Hemi spotted his squad, grabbed a homebrewed beer from the buckets near the door, and headed their way.

They were a scary bunch of badasses. Big, tough, inked…and he'd never fought with a better team.

His brother, Tane, was sprawled in a chair, cradling a beer between his knees. He had his dreadlocks pulled back at the base of his neck, and his gaze was angled toward the dance floor. It looked like he was brooding.

Brooding was standard MO for Hemi's little bro. Tane had seen too much in the jungles of South America, working as a mercenary. Hemi had eventually gone to work with him, specializing in kidnap-victim recovery. They'd lost a few, and rescued a few who'd never be the same…hell, some of the stuff they'd seen was enough to turn Hemi's iron gut.

Still, nothing was as bad as the horrors the Gizzida cooked up in their labs.

Hemi turned his head to follow Tane's gaze. It didn't take him long to find the pretty little silver-haired woman. Their resident alien was dancing with the teens, her skin and hair glowing under the bright lights.

Selena had pale, silver-white hair, and even paler skin. Tonight, someone had decked her out in a glittery blue dress, and she was smiling. He grinned. The woman had no rhythm at all, but it looked like she was having fun. She was another person snatched by the raptors and abused, but since the squads had rescued her, she was slowly blooming. He couldn't imagine how it felt to be so far from your planet and everything you knew, with no way home.

Hemi looked back at his brother. Yes, Selena was blooming and his jaded, hard-ass brother seemed to be very aware of that. *Interesting.*

The rest of his squad mates were gathered nearby. Ash Connors was leaning against the wall, his colored ink displayed by the rolled-up sleeves of his dark shirt. The women fucking loved the man's pretty face, but for some reason, he was solo tonight. Come to think of it, Ash had been showing up solo for a while now.

Ash's best friend, Levi King, was sitting near his friend, a pretty, giggling schoolteacher in his lap. Levi's hair was pulled up in the man bun they all gave him hell for, and he was grinning indulgently at the woman.

The other two berserkers, Griff and Dom, were talking quietly. A couple of women were eying the two, trying to get up the courage to approach them. Hemi snorted. Yeah, good luck with that. The former cop and ex-con, and the former mafia enforcer were dangerous and moody as hell. He knew they fucked women when it suited them, but for the most part, they enjoyed doing the chasing.

His friends all fought hard, partied hard, and did whatever the fuck they wanted.

He scanned the room, trying to see if anyone from Squad Nine had arrived.

"Hey, Hemi."

A beautiful woman who barely reached his shoulder moved in close to him. Her dangerous curves were packed into a red dress and a cloud of dark hair curled around her face. He stifled a sigh. He'd fooled around with Sal a few times at Blue Mountain Base and she'd made it clear she wanted to take it further. The woman was nothing, if not persistent.

"Hey, Sal."

"Got any plans tonight?" She stroked her hand down his arm. "I'd like to rock your world to welcome in the new year."

"Generous, but I've got plans." He scanned the room again. Big plans.

Sal pouted, but nodded. Casual sex wasn't frowned on since the invasion. In a world gone to hell, where so many people had lost their loved ones, being close to someone was sometimes the only thing that helped get people through the long, dark nights.

And living confined in such a small space, people were forced into close proximity.

"Have a good one," he told her.

She looked back over her shoulder. "You're missing out." She blew him a kiss.

He sat down beside Tane and his brother raised a brow. "You have plans?"

"Yep." Hemi sipped his beer.

From behind him, Levi snorted. "About time.

Your balls must be blue by now, Rahia."

Hemi shot the man a finger. "You seem very worried about my balls, King."

Levi smiled. "We all know which sexy Amazon you're panting after. Can't say I blame you."

Hemi lunged out of his chair, but Tane grabbed his arm and yanked him back down.

Levi didn't even flinch. The man's grin just widened, and he sipped his drink.

Hemi knew his friend was just yanking his chain. He sat back, waiting and watching. He tried to calculate how long it would take Squad Nine to get back, and then shower and change. All around him, people were dancing and laughing and drinking. He spied a couple kissing wildly in a shadowed corner.

Finally, he saw Roth enter, with his arm around his partner, Avery. They headed over to where Hell Squad was hanging out.

Anticipation licked at Hemi's gut. She'd be here soon.

Next up, he saw Mac and Taylor appear. Both the women were looking gorgeous in slick little dresses of bronze and green, respectively. Mac made a beeline towards Niko, the Enclave's civilian leader. The man yanked his woman in for a hard kiss. Taylor was only a few steps behind, heading toward her man, Devlin.

Theron and Sienna appeared. The couple had only just tumbled head-over-ass in love, and they'd done it in the middle of a dangerous mission. Hemi and his squad had been there to help rescue them from the middle of an alien encampment. Theron kept a possessive arm around Sienna, who looked cute as hell in a red dress with spots on it. They had a glow about them that said they'd done more than shower after getting back from their mission.

And then there she was.

Cam stepped into the room, looking around.

Holy fuck. What the fuck was she wearing? Hemi's hands tightened on his beer. She was wearing a black dress, but there was nothing simple about it. The hemline was short, showcasing her absolutely fabulous legs. On top of that, the neckline dipped low in front, practically to her waist, and was covered in some sort of silver beads that shimmered in the light.

It was too easy to imagine his hand bunching up that tiny skirt and wrapping those long legs of hers around his hips.

He took another sip of his drink.

Hell yeah, tonight she was his.

Hell Squad

Marcus
Cruz
Gabe
Reed
Roth
Noah
Shaw
Holmes
Niko
Finn
Devlin
Theron
Hemi

MORE ACTION ROMANCE?

**ACTION
ADVENTURE
TREASURE HUNTS
SEXY SCI-FI ROMANCE**

When astro-archeologist and museum curator Dr. Lexa Carter discovers a secret map to a lost old Earth treasure—a priceless Fabergé egg—she's excited at the prospect of a treasure hunt to the dangerous desert planet of Zerzura. What she's not so happy about is being saddled with a bodyguard—the museum's mysterious new head of security, Damon Malik.

After many dangerous years as a galactic spy, Damon Malik just wanted a quiet job where no one tried to kill him. Instead of easy work in a museum full of artifacts, he finds himself on a backwater planet babysitting the most infuriating woman he's ever met.

She thinks he's arrogant. He thinks she's a trouble-magnet. But among the desert sands and ruins, adventure led by a young, brash treasure hunter named Dathan Phoenix, takes a deadly turn. As it becomes clear that someone doesn't want them to find the treasure, Lexa and Damon will have to trust each other just to survive.

The Phoenix Adventures
Among Galactic Ruins
At Star's End
In the Devil's Nebula
On a Rogue Planet
Beneath a Trojan Moon
Beyond Galaxy's Edge
On a Cyborg Planet
Return to Dark Earth
On a Barbarian World
Lost in Barbarian Space
Through Uncharted Space

Also by Anna Hackett

Treasure Hunter Security
Undiscovered
Uncharted
Unexplored
Unfathomed

Galactic Gladiators
Gladiator
Warrior
Hero
Protector
Champion

Hell Squad
Marcus
Cruz
Gabe
Reed
Roth
Noah
Shaw
Holmes
Niko
Finn
Devlin
Theron
Hemi

The Anomaly Series
Time Thief
Mind Raider
Soul Stealer
Salvation
Anomaly Series Box Set

The Phoenix Adventures
Among Galactic Ruins
At Star's End
In the Devil's Nebula
On a Rogue Planet
Beneath a Trojan Moon
Beyond Galaxy's Edge
On a Cyborg Planet
Return to Dark Earth
On a Barbarian World
Lost in Barbarian Space
Through Uncharted Space

Perma Series
Winter Fusion

The WindKeepers Series
Wind Kissed, Fire Bound
Taken by the South Wind
Tempting the West Wind
Defying the North Wind
Claiming the East Wind

Standalone Titles
Savage Dragon
Hunter's Surrender
One Night with the Wolf

Anthologies
A Galactic Holiday
Moonlight (UK only)
Vampire Hunter (UK only)
Awakening the Dragon (UK Only)

For more information visit AnnaHackettBooks.com

About the Author

I'm a USA Today bestselling author and I'm passionate about *action romance*. I love stories that combine the thrill of falling in love with the excitement of action, danger and adventure. I'm a sucker for that moment when the team is walking in slow motion, shoulder-to-shoulder heading off into battle.

I write about people overcoming unbeatable odds and achieving seemingly impossible goals. I like to believe it's possible for all of us to do the same.

My books are mixture of action, adventure and sexy romance and they're recommended for anyone who enjoys fast-paced stories where the boy wins the girl at the end (or sometimes the girl wins the boy!)

For release dates, action romance info, free books, and other fun stuff, sign up for the latest news here:

Website: AnnaHackettBooks.com

81170702R00145

Made in the USA
Columbia, SC
17 November 2017